Promises
of Murder

A.M. Holloway

eBook ISBN: 978-1-7359152-4-1

Paper ISBN: 978-1-7359152-5-8

Library of Congress Control Number: 2021906798

Printed in the United States of America.

Prologue

"Sheriff Steele," I answer my phone as I wipe the sleep out of my eyes. "Come again? You're breaking up on me." The caller expresses the need for my presence at a roadside scene. What could be on Shallow Bottoms Road? There is nothing of significance out there. I slide a coffee mug from my cup tree, add a dash of sweetener and creamer, and then fill my favorite mug with hot coffee from my coffee bar. On my way out the door, I grab a protein bar and set out for the other end of nowhere.

One sip of coffee, and my senses come alive. I can't explain how coffee does it, but everything wakes when the hot liquid spills down my throat. By the time I reach my destination, I've enjoyed half of my coffee. I place my mug in the console and slide the lid in place, hoping it will save a little heat for my next drive.

The scene is crawling with people when I park next to Deputy Taylor's patrol car. Blue and red lights flash, unlike anything I've seen in the past. Every on-duty law enforcement officer in the county must be here. My deputy leans against his car until he sees me get out of mine. Sgt Taylor swaggers over to me and says, "Sheriff, we have a problem."

3

"Taylor, I assumed that is why you called me in the middle of the night. So, what's the situation?" I survey the area while waiting for Sgt Taylor's reply. Nothing of consequence shows its face, yet.

"You need to see it, Sheriff. A description will not suffice on this one," Sgt Taylor directs me towards the ditch and points to the find. He shines a flashlight for me to see the way.

As I peer over the edge of the ditch, I take a minute to decipher what I am seeing. The ditch is about three feet deep, a few feet wide, and used for water runoff. This barely traveled road sits on the outskirts of the county. It's a one-lane road used mainly as a cut-through for local people saving time during dry weather. Once this road gets wet, it becomes so slick drivers have a hard time keeping their cars on it. There have been many accidents on this road.

Jumping down into the ditch, I draw a breath when I get close enough to make out the scene. The eyes of three dead girls stare back at me. The girls appear to be no more than seventeen years old. It's possible they are younger but dressed to appear older. Someone shot all three in the head execution style, bound, gagged, and dumped them in my county.

"Taylor, who found these girls? It's time I speak with them." I ask as I climb out of the ditch. When I look down, I notice dirt covers my pants legs. I grimace. It's impossible to

4

climb out of that ditch and remain clean. I rubbed my hands together to release what little dirt I could.

"Sheriff, there is a car parked down the road with a boy and girl inside. The boy called it in to 911. We told them you would want to speak with them about the discovery." Taylor explains.

"Thanks, I'll go see them now. You were right about this being odd. If no one has called the medical examiner yet, do it." With more dirt remaining on my hands. I wipe them down my pants as I walk over to the car holding the kids. "Oh, and Taylor, keep people away from the ditch."

The driver, a teenage boy, sees me approaching and exits the car. He is visibly distraught to the point his body trembles. "Hi, I'm Sheriff Steele. Thanks for hanging out until I could get here. Can you tell me how you found the girls?" The female passenger stays in the car, bawling her eyes out. I don't make her get out because she couldn't offer any information until her crying stops, anyway.

The boy speaks in a shaky voice, "We, my girlfriend and I, were cutting through on our way home when we saw a box truck stopped in the middle of the road. As we get closer, a guy dropped the back door on the truck and then sped away. I saw no tag on the back of the truck or any markings on the side when he turned the corner. We thought it was weird to stop in the road, so I pulled over where they parked, got out, and found the girls in the ditch. Now, I wish I would have taken another way home." The boy lowers his head as he stares at his shaking hands.

The box truck bothers me. "You mentioned the truck had no markings, right? So, you're saying there wasn't a company name or anything on it, right? So, what can you tell me about the truck's color?"

"Yes. That's right, no markings, and it was solid white except for the dirt. The truck stood out as strange since it had no markings on it. I've never seen one like that around here."

"Go on home, and if we need you, we will call. Thanks again." I shake his hand and pass him a business card.

The boy leaves the scene, and I can tell neither one of those kids will ever forget tonight. My prayer is they survive the nightmares that come with witnessing something so gruesome.

Chapter 1

My name is Sheriff Jada Ivey Steele, and my dad was the county sheriff before me. I grew up with him without a mom. She left us when I was two months old. We never heard from her again, or at least I didn't. So, it was just my dad and me. Law enforcement is in my blood. Dad talked about his job and what it meant to him. So, all the while, I grew up knowing I would pursue a career in law enforcement.

A drunk guy shot my dad point-blank in the chest when dad stopped him in the middle of town. Dad died in the street. He never had a chance. Back in those days, the sheriff's office didn't have the money for bulletproof vests, and the deputies couldn't afford them on their own, so they went without protection. Dad died a hero that day. The county people loved him. Council members from all over the county approached me the day after I laid him to rest, wanting me to run for his position. Back then, I was a patrol officer, trying to learn my way. A week later, I agreed.

No one ran against me in the first sheriff's election. Maybe they felt sorry for me. So far, I've survived two elections. A female in a man's position is difficult at first, but you learn how to handle people quickly. A pushover, I am not. However, growing up with a sheriff for a dad, you learned how to be tough. Kids in school were not always the nicest, so I turned to sports to keep me out of trouble. It turns out I was an above-average basketball player. Basketball helped me make it through school, and when I left high school for college, I gave up basketball for criminal justice. Dad tried to talk me out of law enforcement, but I wouldn't let it go, so he hired me.

Chapter 2

"Hey, Doc. Come on in and take a seat. Tell me what you have on the girls." I offer the medical examiner a seat across from my desk.

"How are you, Sheriff Steele? Rough night, huh?" He asks as he struggles to sit.

"Not the greatest I've ever had. It would be helpful if the crime scene gave us some evidence. I didn't notice any in the ditch last night."

"Yes, I understand. Well, unfortunately, I cannot offer you much in the evidence collection either. All three girls were shot, which you saw, and none carried ID. We found no cell phones or purses in the ditch or the immediate area. So far, we are looking at missing person lists from Georgia and surrounding states now. My staff and I will have the autopsies completed by the end of the day today. I wanted to share my preliminary report with you."

"Somehow, I figured that's what you would say, but I have to admit I was hoping for more. Thanks, Doc, for coming over. Call me when you finish with the autopsies. I'm eager for those results, and I'll be waiting for the pictures."

Doc James is a massive man, so he takes a little longer than most to leave my office. I watch as he drags his feet over to the front door of the office. As the door closes, I say, "Maggie, come see me, please."

My office assistant has been with me since the beginning. Maggie and I went to high school together. She married her high school boyfriend, and when I won the election, she begged to come to work with me. I'm glad she did. Maggie keeps me straight, and that is no easy feat.

"Yes, Sheriff," Maggie says as she enters my office.

"Have we had any reports of suspicious box trucks around town? Like at the diners, hotels, anywhere? A witness spotted a dirty white box truck at the murder scene and we need to locate it."

"Not that I know of, Sheriff, but I'll check with dispatch on the box truck. Do we have photos of the deceased parties yet? I'll add them to the federal database."

"No pictures yet but let me know what you find out on the box truck. It's our only lead. Thanks, Maggie." I am at a loss with only one lead on an unidentifiable box truck.

I spin my desk chair around and stare out the window. Why would three dead girls be in a ditch in my county? No one at the scene recognized the girls, so I am assuming they are out-of-towners. But from where? If they are from out of town, how did the driver know about Shallow Bottoms Road? My county has just as many dirt roads as it does paved ones.

We live in the deep south and off a beaten path. Not much happens here. Our county sits one county away from Interstate 75, which runs north and south through Georgia, and one county north of Florida. It is roughly 350 square miles, so some roads remain without a regular patrol. Shallow Bottoms Road would fall into that category.

Maggie closes my office door as commotion ensues in the hallway, and I hope it stays out there. Quiet time is a treasure around here. Could today get any worse? I have three unidentified dead girls lying in the county morgue and no leads.

I say, "come in," to the door knocker after a slight tap on the door. My solitude didn't last long, so I roll my shoulders, waiting for the exchange.

"Sheriff, I'm with K4TV, and I would like to ask a few questions about the overnight murders. I realize I am early, but we would appreciate anything you can share." The black-haired lady stands erect in my doorway. She is all business, but I feel a niggle creep up my spine. How did she hear about the bodies so fast?

I take a breath and stand up from my chair. "I'm not ready to give a press release. The autopsies are not complete yet. We will notify the media when we schedule a press conference. So, please, leave." I sit down in my chair, hoping she gets the message. But no.

"Just one statement, Sheriff. Give the public something," the reporter begs.

"I answered your questions. When I have more, we will notify you. Now, I'm asking politely one more time. Next time might not be so polite. Please, leave the office."

She turns in a huff and marches out the door. As she turns the corner, I see her heading to Maggie's desk. To stop her, I race out of my office, and before she says anything, she sees me approaching. Thinking twice about a rebuttal, she leaves the office building without uttering another word.

Maggie's eyes shift from me to the news reporter and back again. I didn't explain, and she didn't ask, so I returned to my office.

The surprise visit by the press rattles me. The media is not my friend. They always seem to tweak my words and not the way I intend. When I am ready, I will give a press conference. Doc James should have information later today. Three autopsies take time, and the press will have to wait for the results for once. The thought of how they knew about the murders so soon is troublesome. Is someone in my department divulging critical information?

Time is not on my side. Murders are notoriously hard to solve the longer they linger unsolved. But where to start? Three girls, not local, shot, bound, and gagged. Is this gang-related? We have some activity, but it's been just kids stealing from other kids so far, maybe a little graffiti, but nothing violent. Other counties have more violent gangs, but they haven't reached us yet. It can't hurt to call around and see if any nearby counties have had similar activity. If any county in South Georgia had similar murders, someone would have notified me, but I want to check myself.

The county has traffic accidents, thefts, domestics—the lightweight stuff. Our department is configured differently from other sheriff departments across the state. Since we have such a sparse population, our department doesn't have dedicated investigators. Instead, we cross-train our patrol deputies for investigations. The first on-scene deputy is the lead investigator. Lucky for me, it was Sgt Taylor this time. He's the best of the best.

"Sgt Taylor, report to my office. Bring your report from the murder scene." I call his desk phone in the bullpen. Not sure who named the room, but it stuck. The bullpen is a rectangular room, and it houses all the deputies. Each deputy has a desk, computer, printer, and a landline phone. The sheriff's department also provides portable radios for each deputy to wear on their shoulders. The radios connect to the county 911 system, dispatching for the sheriff's department, fire department, and ambulance calls.

While I wait, I add notes to my notebook. I have every notebook since the first day I took office. These have become invaluable

13

in several instances, especially in court. I store the notebooks in a secret place because I can't take the chance someone or something might cause them harm.

"Come in, Sgt Taylor. Take a seat." I answer a rap on my door.

As Taylor sits, I look at him. He is younger than me by a few years, stocky, a high school football player. Deputy Damon Taylor is book smart and street smart, which makes him a fantastic deputy to have on my roster. Also, someone to train the rookies too. "Any updates yet?"

"No, Sheriff. Last night's report is complete. We have found no one who has seen a truck like what the witness described. If the kid had taken a different road, it's possible no one would have found those girls. It's such a shame." Sgt Taylor turns his eyes downward.

Since I am taken aback by Sgt Taylor's comment, I pause before I answer. "You are right. It is a shame these girls ended up in a ditch. These girls have a family, and I am certain someone misses them. Doc James will have the autopsies today for all three girls. If you need a nap, get it now. We will meet at the medical examiner's office for the rundown on the autopsies once they are complete. Maggie will add the girls to the federal database for us. So, between the autopsy and the federal database, we should have their names. Anything else you want to mention?"

"Nothing comes to mind until we see the autopsies except the gunshot wound appears to be a 9mm caliber bullet, based on the wounds' size. However, Doc James will confirm that before I add it to the report." Sgt Taylor looks down and skims his report, looking for anything else he missed. There is nothing to add, so he excuses himself and exits my office.

My mind wanders to Sgt Taylor. He rarely acts like this. On a typical day, he is cocky and annoying. Today, he is quiet and somewhat subdued. I hope he feels like he can confide in me if something is bothering him. Maybe seeing those girls lying in a ditch stirred his emotions. We don't get crime scenes like that in our county, and that makes it more difficult.

After Taylor left my office, I took a moment to contact some nearby sheriff's. A few I spoke with were already aware of the murders. However, not one gave me a lead. They did, however, agree to add the box truck to their lookout sheets. No other sheriff has experienced anything like these murders either. Apparently, I was alone again.

As I raise my head, I notice the whiteboard on my wall. We haven't used the board for a criminal investigation in months, maybe a year. The markers are inside my desk—somewhere. After rummaging through two drawers, I find them crammed in the back of the third one. Once I close the door to my office, I list each dead girl on the board and her description using a red marker. The girls did not look alike, other than being similar in age. I cannot find any other physical similarities. Doc James would confirm the bullet caliber, type of zip ties used to restrain the girls, and anything else he saw to help solve these murders. So I wait.

After I cover the whiteboard in information, I step back and stare at the descriptions. The data doesn't help me uncover a reason for the bodies to be in my county. The only connection between the victims is how they died, and the zip ties used to restrain them. Everything else is different about them-different clothes, hair, and eye color. So, what connects these girls?

My phone rings, and I reach over and snatch it from the cradle without checking the caller ID. "Sheriff Steele," I cringe as I listen to the caller.

"Sheriff, I'm Ned Cates, K4TV. Don't hang up. The reason for the call is to apologize for the earlier interruption from my reporter. She explained how upset you were. After what I heard, you had every right to be upset. Finding bodies in a ditch should shake everyone's core."

"Who told you there were bodies in a ditch?" I ask sternly.

"Uh. I can't say how I found out, but you confirmed it. Thanks for that. Is there any information you can share with the media? We

16

haven't received a notice of a scheduled press conference by your office."

"That's because I haven't scheduled one. The sheriff's department will notify the media when we schedule one. Goodbye." I place the phone back on the cradle without breaking it, and I am proud of myself for that small test of restraint. The media drives me crazy. Maybe Ned will sit in the front row at the conference. That should be fun.

Since Doc James hasn't called with the results of the autopsies, I take myself to lunch. There is a lot of planning to do, but I'm uncertain where to begin until we receive more information on the victims. Whoever did this to these poor young girls, I want to meet the killer face to face. I want to see what kind of person it takes to kill a defenseless young person.

The best diner in town will be busy at this time of the day. My lunch begins earlier than most, so I can get in and out in a reasonable time, but not today. As I enter, the townspeople wave at me to stop at their table. I politely nod and walk towards the counter to place a takeout order since so many patrons fill the restaurant. The cook walks over and asks, "Sheriff, what can I cook for you today?"

"Anything on the menu that is quick. I should have gone home for lunch. At least I would have been alone." I wink while explaining my haste to leave the diner.

"Give me a second, and the food will be

ready in a jiff." The cook disappears and returns in a flash. He hands me a takeout box and says it is on the house today.

Shaking my head, "I appreciate it, but I can't do that." I lay money on the counter and turn to exit the diner. People call my name, and I wave on my way out the door. I'm grateful when the door shuts behind me. Rude people irritate me. It's a shame a person can't enjoy lunch. There is not enough time to speak with each person in the diner. If I had, I would spend the rest of the day repeating myself. They elected me as sheriff because I am approachable, but not today because I have a pressing matter waiting for attention.

The drive back to the office is too short, so I pull behind the building and enjoy a quiet lunch as I listen to the radio crackle in my police-issued vehicle. My deputies patrol the county, and the dispatchers monitor the situations. Everyone is on edge as we search for a killer.

After I finish lunch, a call comes over the radio. "Deputy Tuttle for Sheriff Steele."

Grabbing the mic, I key it, "Sheriff Steele here. What's up, Tuttle?"

"Can you meet me at the Snappy Mart on Route 3?"

"10-4 Tuttle." Wonder what he found? I ask myself as I activate the lights and siren. Route 3 is a busy road, as is the Snappy Mart, because people visit the store at all hours. It's one of only a few that are open twenty-four hours a day. Please don't let there be another body. We are still waiting to hear from the medical examiner on the three victims from overnight.

The Snappy Mart isn't overly busy when I enter the lot. I turned the lights and siren off about a mile back because I didn't want to draw attention to the scene if there is one. The owner has his back towards the door as he speaks with Deputy Tuttle. Tuttle waves at me to come on over. The store owner looks at me with a worried expression.

"Hey, Sal. What's wrong?" I direct the question to the owner.

"Hi, Sheriff. My lab, Roxy, joins me at the store most mornings. She went out to do her business a little while ago, and she comes back with that." He points over to his desk in the back room.

Glancing at Deputy Tuttle, I walk to the desk and study the item. It is a tennis shoe, only one, the right one. It is a Nike brand, a gray shoe with a black Nike emblem on it.

"Tuttle, bag the item into evidence, and be careful not to smudge the stain. There is a possibility it is blood. We will check and see if it matches one of our bodies at the morgue." Tuttle stands ready as he produces an evidence bag and gloves.

"Sal, do you use surveillance cameras in your store? We are searching for the person responsible for killing those girls we found on Shallow Bottoms Road."

"Yeah, I heard. That's why I spoke to Deputy Tuttle when he came in for coffee. I thought you should check out the shoe. The store has one camera, and it points towards the gas pumps in case of drive-offs. We can check it and see if we spot someone suspicious."

"Thanks, Sal. That would be great to see the video. By the way, what direction did Roxy take this morning? Might help us locate more items." I jot a few notes in my book.

"Roxy runs to the right about twenty yards and circles back to the left and then back inside. Her routine takes her about 10-15 minutes, depending on the weather. Roxy has been doing that since she was a pup. Give me a minute, and I'll cue the video for you, Sheriff."

I walk over to Deputy Tuttle and quietly say, "We will search the area. See if you can wrestle up help. Anyone will do. Johnson's tracking dog might be of service, if he wants to come in for overtime."

Tuttle trots back to his vehicle to work on his assignment. It impresses me when I realize Tuttle makes calls with his cell phone instead of his radio. He hasn't been a deputy for a long time, but he picks up fast. The media hasn't figured out how to eavesdrop on our cell phones yet. At least, we can keep them away for a little while longer.

"Sheriff, the video is ready for you.

Come get me when you finish." Sal walks to the front of the store as I stroll to the back.

"Thanks, Sal." I plop myself into his worn leather chair and start the video. The store has frequent gas customers. No box trucks were at the pumps, but what is that on the top of the screen? It looks like it might be a truck. "Hey, Sal, can you come in here?" I yell out the door, hoping he can hear me.

"Sure, Sheriff. What's up?" Sal walks over to his desk.

"Sal, see the image up there on the top of the screen? Is there a way to zoom in on it or check another angle?"

"Sheriff, there isn't another angle. That's the only camera I have. Although, after this, I plan on adding additional cameras to the store. I wish I were more help."

"You did good, Sal. A few of us will search out back for more items. Try to keep the public away if you can. Thanks again for your help." I stand and pat Sal's shoulder.

When I exit his store, Tuttle stands behind his vehicle, gathering gear for our hike. He turns towards me and says, "Sheriff, Johnson is reporting in with Rufus. He will be here in ten minutes."

"Ok. I'll be ready. Don't leave without me." I reply as my car door closes. Then I take a deep breath. This case is zapping all my energy, but I must make the call. "Doc James, Sheriff Steele speaking. We are at the Snappy

Mart, and the owner's dog brought us a shoe. It is a girl's size sneaker. Once we finish with the search of the area, I will head your way. If I bring it by your place, would you be available to check and see if the shoe fits one of our girls?"

"Absolutely I can, Sheriff. We will complete the autopsies by the time you get here too. I will be waiting."

"Thanks, Doc." I end the call and glance at the store. The Snappy Mart is an out-of-the-way place to stop for someone in hiding. The truck in the video didn't pump gas, so the driver must have gone inside for something. I need to question Sal to find out who worked the hours before and after someone dumped the girls. Once I write the reminder in my book, Johnson pulls alongside my car with Rufus grinning through the window.

The three of us gather behind Tuttle's car and share the information we received from Sal with Deputy Johnson. Tuttle produces the shoe, and Johnson instructs Rufus to work. The dog sniffs the shoe for a few seconds, and then he sits down at Johnson's feet. Rufus is Johnson's family dog because the department doesn't have the funds to pay for a tracking dog. If we did, Rufus would be it. He helps us frequently track down missing kids, along with a few older adults. I love that dog.

Johnson and Rufus take the lead, and we follow. Rufus runs, and all the while, his nose is to the ground. He stops twice for water, then off

22

again we go. It feels like we cover the same territory twice, but Johnson corrects me. We walked in a wide arc. Johnson explains Sal provided a map of Roxy's walking path, and then he expanded the area to give Rufus a chance to zero in on a specific spot. An hour after the hike first started, Rufus did his strange growl. He found something.

Chapter 3

Rufus found something all right. He located the matching tennis shoe Roxy brought Sal. As we examine the shoe, we spot a scrap of material that wedged itself into the shoelaces. "Bag the shoe. Let's keep walking in the same direction. Look around on our walk back to see if we find anything else. Rufus, you did good, boy!" I shower Rufus with serious petting and a belly rub.

Our walk back turns fruitless. No one finds anything useful. Once we return to our vehicles, I advise the guys I'm going to the medical examiner's office for the autopsy results and try these shoes on our girls. The shoes will fit at least one girl, I imagine. Both deputies agree with me on the footwear. Not that it proves anything, but it will add information to the murder board.

With the pair of sneakers in my front seat, I drive to Doc James' office. It is in the basement of the city hall. The entrance is in the back lot. Not sure why, but it has been since I was a little girl. So, I pull around back and park beside Deputy Taylor. After our greeting, we walk through the unlocked door. The walls and the floors are a light gray color with black chairs. I will never understand why our medical examiners do not add a splash of color to their offices. It would make visiting more somewhat enjoyable.

"Hey, Doc. Here are the shoes I called you about earlier." I lifted the bags toward Doc James. Taylor eyed them as I passed them to the doctor.

"You're right. These are a small size. Let's start with victim one and see if they fit."

We walk over to the metal tables in the room's center. Each female lies on a table with her hair combed away from her face, and a sheet pulled to her neck. Doc James takes his time trying the shoes on each girl. Girl number three is the winner, as the shoes fit her perfectly. "What was she wearing, Doc?"

Doc James steps over to his desk eyeing his computer as an email alert sounded. "Victim three wore a white skirt with a pullover shirt as tennis players wear on the court."

"The sneakers make sense then if she wore a tennis skirt. But why would she dress in tennis attire?" I share glances with Taylor and Doc James.

"I can't answer that, Sheriff. But the results are ready. You two take a seat." Doc waves his arm out toward the chairs. He has a black chair I always sit in, and it is ready for today's visit. Taylor slides another chair over closer to the desk. Doc James pulls his files up on the computer and reads them aloud as we take notes. He states, "Someone sexually abused all three girls, and they each had ligature marks around their wrists and ankles. Two girls had cuts on the sides of their mouths, showing someone gagged them for long periods. The cause of death is a close-range gunshot wound to the frontal lobe of the brain. Someone shot each girl with a 9MM bullet from a handgun. All three girls have exit wounds at the back of the head, and we did not find bullet fragments to use for comparison. The ditch provided a dumpsite, but it was not the kill site."

"So, did we recover any forensic evidence we can use to identify these girls?" I question with a head tilt.

"Sheriff, we collected the clothes, the zip ties, and I found one strand of hair that didn't match the girls. Hardware stores across the country sell these zip ties. My assistant is locating the seller of the clothes. However, I expect little. They didn't look expensive, just ordinary. A suggestion would be to enter the girls into the national database and hope for a hit. The bodies will remain here until someone claims them. The DNA results on the strand of hair are not back yet. Those won't be available until tomorrow."

"So much for evidence. I was hoping to have something to go on, that's all. Sorry if I sound mad. I am, but not at you. Thanks for getting these done so fast. Maggie will enter their information into the system today." The doctor reaches his hand over the desk, and I shake it, then we let ourselves out of his office. The office is eerily quiet to the point of being unnerving, and I can't wait to get outside. I do a little speed walking to make a hasty exit as Taylor chuckles behind me. He knows I hate the medical examiner's office, and I don't know why.

Sitting in my car, I try to clear my head. This case is challenging, to say the least. Since the citizens elected me sheriff, we have not had unsolved cases. Now, I must admit, we have had no murders in our county either. So, I don't want my first murder to go unsolved. I pledge to myself we will solve this case. However, I don't put a time frame on it.

On my way back to the department, I notify the other deputies by cell phone to report to the bullpen in thirty minutes for a meeting. They need updating on the autopsy results, which isn't much. When I walk in the door, I have just enough time to hand Maggie the information required to enter the girls' information into the federal database. She agrees to handle the entries personally before she leaves for the day. This case bothers her too. She wants justice for these girls as badly as I do.

The bullpen hops with activity when I arrive. Everyone is eager to hear the news. "Thanks for coming so quickly. I wanted to share the updates we've received over the past few hours. The autopsies are complete, and someone shot the victims at close range with a single 9MM bullet. Each victim has an exit wound, and there are no bullet fragments for comparison. Someone sexually abused the victims, and their bodies have ligature marks on their ankles and wrists. Two victims have marks on the sides of their mouths, showing the killer gagged them for an extended period. Deputy Tuttle stopped at the Snappy Mart, and Sal, the owner, explained how his dog, Roxy, brought him a sneaker. We hiked the same area with Rufus, and we found the match for the sneaker. Doc James found the owner of the sneakers belonging to one of our females. Although the shoes don't help with finding the killer, they provide a lead. Identification of the victims remains unknown, so Maggie is entering their descriptions into the federal database before leaving for the night. I know that was a lot and quick, so what questions do you have?"

Deputy Johnson speaks up first, "Have we received the Georgia missing person list yet?"

"Yes, and the victims match none of the females on the list, leading us to a dead end. We can request lists from surrounding states, but that takes time and resources. I want to wait until Maggie enters the information into the federal database. The entries will expedite the results from the inquiries. If someone enters them tonight, we will start with the requests first thing in the morning. Everyone is tired. I know I am. So, those who have already worked twenty-four hours go home. I will spend the night in the office in case anything happens."

The deputies clear out of the bullpen and leave me sitting at my desk. I enjoy my alone time as it gives me space to sort out ideas without explaining my reasons. Writing possibilities on the board helps me visualize our next move to find the killer. As I sit in my chair, my eyes grow heavy. I will my body to move to the sofa before I fall asleep at my desk.

Someone taps me on the shoulder, and as I open my eyes slowly, I stare at Maggie.

"Sheriff, wake up. It's morning. Did you spend the night here?" Maggie questions.

"What? Is it morning already? I laid down for a minute." I stammer.

"Here is a cup of coffee. The next shift change is in fifteen minutes. Where is your extra change of clothes? You're looking a little rumpled." Maggie says with a sincere grin on her face.

Looking down at my clothes, it appears I had slept in them. "Oh, my word. My shirt has more wrinkles than I can count. I have extra clothes in the bathroom closet. Thanks, Maggie. What would I do without you?"

Maggie glances over her shoulder and says, "Let's not find out, shall we?"

I change clothes and try to make myself somewhat presentable for the day. A hot shower is on my to-do list today. My body aches all over from sleeping crooked on that horrible piece of furniture I call a sofa. Every time I sleep on it, I threaten to dump it.

My entire department sits in the bullpen when I enter. They look like I feel. Beat up, sad, and no answers in sight. "Good morning. No news came in overnight as no one spotted the box truck. We will wait for information from the federal database. Go on patrol for those on duty. If you're not on the roster for today, go home and try to rest. You are to be readily available, so keep cell phones handy. Dispatch will call your cells too. Only cell phones for communication during the murder investigation. The media are after me for an update, and I'm trying to hold them off until I get something solid. If the media seeks you out, refer them to me. Questions?"

Since no one speaks up, we leave and prepare for the day the best we can. Maggie stands at my office door with a stack of paper. "Here are phone messages that came in for you, Sheriff. Most are from the media requesting a news conference. Doc James left a message overnight, stating the hair he found was not enough to test for DNA. A few messages were from residents wanting an update because they're scared to let their kids play outside. Want me to return the calls from the media for you? I'll tell them you are working on a conference and will call them with a time and date."

"Please do. That will stall them for a

little while, anyway. I want to check in with the federal database this morning. Surely, these girls are on the list. They appeared well cared for, so I can only imagine what their families are going through." Maggie walks towards her desk with the stack of messages. She does not understand how much I depend on her.

My computer sits on my desk, waiting for me to start the searches. I turn it on and log into the federal database and take a deep breath. Time stands still as I carefully enter a specific search for each victim. It feels like it takes forever, but I have no idea where to start. The realization hits when I decide these girls might be from any state in the United States. I'm still wondering how they ended up dumped in my county.

While the database search does its thing, I review yesterday's reports from my deputies. Nothing appears significant as it relates to our active case. We had one fender bender, one potential theft, and a missing cat reported. So, yesterday was more or less uneventful.

"Sheriff, we received a hit on the girls," Maggie states matter-of-factly.

"How? I received nothing from my federal database search I entered a while ago." I reply as I run my fingers through my hair.

Maggie explains, "Last night, as I entered the information, I flagged it for possibilities, not exact matches. An email came in a moment ago, and I forwarded it to you."

"Let's read it together." I slide the papers over on my desk and click my email icon. The latest email received has an FBI email address. I glance up at Maggie as I open it. We take a minute to read through the email because I am not sure how to react. "Did you read our girls might be part of a serial killer operating in the southeastern states of the country?"

"Yes, Sheriff. That is exactly what I read! Thank goodness you didn't give a news conference yesterday. With the recent information, everyone will go berserk. Do you think the killer is still in our county, or did he drive through and dump the victims?"

My brain pauses before I answer. "I'm hoping the killer passed through, but the questions are: where were they going, where did they come from, and where are they now? The FBI email states someone from the agency will contact us directly. Let me know when they do."

"Will do, Sheriff. Hope it is sooner rather than later with the unease the situation is creating in the county." Maggie states as she returns to her desk.

The FBI email is short, which leads me to believe the investigation is more serious than I ever imagined. When I saw the three bodies, something niggled the back of my neck because it was far more severe than what it appeared. At least if it involves the FBI, there is a chance to solve the case quickly.

I leave the office by the back door since

the media vans pack the front parking lot. There is no way I am giving a press release until I speak with the FBI. What kind of person kills young girls and then throws them away like garbage? Hopefully, the FBI has a suspect or two. I stop by home and shower as a precaution. I don't want to meet an FBI agent smelling like yesterday.

During the drive, I notice more out-of-town cars at the diner than usual. Interesting timing. When I back into my driveway, I see a van parked two houses down the road. The van sports a Georgia tag, but I can't read the county name because of the distance. As soon as I put the key in the lock, someone yells my name. I turn around and watch an older woman with white hair running towards me.

"Sheriff, I apologize for ambushing you at home, but you are ignoring the media at your office." The lady scolds, holding her recorder to my mouth.

"Let me stop you right there. Please leave. When there is something to share with the media, I will." I turn my back to the lady without asking her name. However, the reporter puts her hand on my shoulder to halt my progression. That was a mistake. As I turn around, I grab her arm, pinning her against the wall, and call for backup. A deputy can cart her off to a holding cell. My nerves are raw, and I can't take the media anymore. Of course, I will let her out once I return to the office, but sometimes, enough is enough.

Within minutes, Deputy Taylor arrives with lights and sirens. He bolts from his car and races to my position. After I share the issue, Taylor handcuffs the lady with a grin and a wink. Then he ushers her from my front lawn to his waiting patrol car. The reporter sneers at me as she passes my house from the backseat of a patrol car. I should have waved, but I didn't. Once Taylor delivers her to the jail, they place her in a holding cell with instructions not to process her into the system.

The shower I take after the altercation with the reporter is the best one in recent memory. Hot water and steam can melt away tons of anxiety. I am nervous and anxious, waiting for the FBI to call. A change of clothes, a little makeup, and clean hair gives a woman a new outlook. Back in my car, I know I am ready for whatever the rest of the day brings.

"Sheriff, report to the office. The FBI is on the way." Maggie's voice is slightly edgy as she talks on the radio. Maggie is still getting used to the radio even though she has been with me for years. She recently started using it.

"This is Sheriff Steele. Reporting to the office. If the FBI agents beat me there, show them into my office. Is the media lady still in the holding cell?"

"Yes, she is still here waiting for you," Maggie chuckles.

I don't respond as I throw the car into drive and make my way to the office. The lady reporter is furious with me but calms down after we speak. The lesson she has learned today will stick with her forever. After her release, I walk into my office, and I am face to face with a female. She is almost as tall as me and wears her hair the same way. "Hi, I'm Sheriff Steele."

"Nice to meet you." The agent hands over her badge as she says, "I'm FBI Special Agent Lana Nell Ivey."

Her last name catches me by surprise, but I don't stop to inquire about it. "Are you with a partner? I thought the FBI traveled in pairs." I question, looking around for another person.

"Not now. I'm here to see the scene and the victims firsthand. A serial killer is running the south murdering young girls then tossing them. Your group is our fourth, and someone found them shortly after death, which was unusual. The other bodies showed signs of decay before someone found them. We have identified all previous victims. So far, they have lived in Louisiana, Mississippi, and Alabama. All the victims were young girls, found tied and gagged with a bullet to the head. I'm here to compare the others with the ones found in your county. If they match our killer, the troops will arrive shortly."

"Let's get started then. Doc James agreed to meet with us. He is our medical examiner. Do you need to freshen up before we leave?"

Agent Ivey looks around the office and asks, "Where are the facilities? I'll stop in on our way out."

"Right this way." I guide Agent Ivey into the hallway and show her the way.

While waiting for Agent Ivey, I ponder our itinerary. First, we will visit Doc James, and he can share his findings firsthand. Second, we will go to Shallow Bottoms Road, and finally, we will stop in the Snappy Mart, and I'll show her where we discovered the shoe. I doubt the last two stops will boost the investigation, but I want her to see everything.

"Sheriff Steele, I'm ready when you are." Agent Ivey breaks my concentration.

"Maggie, you can reach me on my cell for the rest of the day. If anything comes in, please share." We walk to the car with the news people staring at us. I try to ignore them, so I talk with Agent Ivey.

"How long have you been with the FBI, Agent Ivey?"

"I've been with the FBI for eight years, out of the Louisiana Bureau. Law enforcement has interested me since I was a little girl. In my sophomore year in college, we had a speaker from the FBI in my criminal law class. From then on, I knew I would be an agent someday. I didn't realize I would make the cut right out of school. Testing comes easy, and I'm athletic, so somehow, I made it work. What about you, Sheriff? What's your story? I'm sure you have one. We all do."

Chapter 4

"I'm in my second term as sheriff. My dad was sheriff before me. A drunk man killed him in the line of duty, and the city council asked me to run to fill his vacancy. I did, even though I did not understand what I was doing. A patrol deputy at the time of his murder, I've endured a lot of on-the-job training."

We settle into the car, and I call dispatch, letting them know we'll be at Doc James' office. The ride is pleasant. Agent Ivey answers emails and text messages. Neither of us feels the need to talk unnecessarily. The radio crackles with activity, but I escape a call as we pull into the parking lot. Agent Ivey follows me in the side door, and I notice as she looks around the dull space. "Not much color in here, Sheriff."

"No kidding. This place is as dull as they come. I keep threatening to bring a picture or something with a bold color, but Doc James would have a stroke. Just wait, you'll see what I mean."

Doc James sits in his chair when we enter his office. "Don't get up, Doc. We need to start on the reports. Doc, this is FBI Special Agent Lana Ivey. Lana, meet Doc James."

Agent Ivey leans over the desk and

shakes Doc's hand. From her expression, she understands why I pushed for the Doc to remain seated. "Nice to meet you, Agent Ivey. The reports are ready." Doc James states as his eyes bounce between the two women. He begins in his languid pace, and he covers the same points with Agent Ivey as he did with me. He has nothing new to report. Agent Ivey takes copious notes as her eyebrows bunch up. She states, "By my guess, these victims are the subject of the South's latest serial killer."

My cell phone rings, so I excuse myself to answer the call. Sgt Taylor calls, asking if I could use his help at the Snappy Mart. His eagerness to meet an FBI agent is comical. I cave in and agree for him to meet us. Excitement sounds in his voice. This will be a fun meeting, and I am looking forward to it. By the time I finish my call, Agent Ivey and Doc James conclude the discussion. Agent Ivey stands in the doorway, waiting for me.

"Are you ready for the next stop, Agent Ivey?" A strange pang happens every time I say her name.

"Yes, I am. Our next stop is the road where the witnesses discovered the girls, right?"

"Shallow Bottoms Road. It is a dirt road in the middle of nowhere. I want to find out whether the killer knew about the road or if it was pure luck they found it." I explain as I shake my head, still trying to make sense of the murders.

"Unfortunately, Sheriff, all the other deaths match the killer's MO. Young girls, bound and gagged, shot execution style, and then dumped on the side of a quiet, out-of-the-way road. As you probably gathered, my report will add your girls to the serial killer's victim list. We can help with identification as Doc James said the girls carried no identification with them. Is that true?"

"We found no cell phone or purse for any of the girls. The only item recovered, other than their clothes, are the sneakers. Maggie's waiting for a response from the federal database before we search for their clothing brands. If one victim were wearing a brand sold in a certain state, we could start a search in that state. Although, Doc James didn't have any luck with the clothes."

"Sheriff, kudos to you for your investigative skill. We often overlook the clothes brand as a lead. The FBI has several databases used to find missing people. I submitted the girls to another database for missing kids. Our killer has been snatching girls from one state and dropping them in another. So, you were right in your assumption that these girls could be from anywhere."

The ride to Shallow Bottoms Roads takes twenty minutes from the town's center. We share small talk as she surveys the city on her way out of town. Agent Ivey stops talking when I pull over to the side of the road. She exits the vehicle and does a complete circle. She takes photos from all sides of the road and the ditch. After she climbs down in the ditch, she walks up and down the trench, looking intently with every step. I don't break her concentration, but I wanted to tell her we did the same thing and didn't find a clue. Not that we couldn't have missed something. "This is a strange place to dump the girls. Wonder how the killer found the spot? So far, this is the most secluded dumpsite we've encountered. You said the only way you found them was a young boy and girl driving the road to get home at night."

"That's right. The locals use Shallow Bottoms to cut through to the other side of town. It saves a few minutes, but the road is unusable in inclement weather. The kids pulled in behind the box truck as the driver lowered the back door. We don't think the driver saw them because he jumped into the cab and took off. The young boy gave the truck's description as a small box truck, with no markings or colorings other than it was a dirty white color without a tag." I explain.

"The kids are the only witnesses. If the driver didn't look at them, there would be no way for the kids to be in danger. Just to be safe, I suggest we add extra patrols to their home addresses." Agent Ivey suggests.

"Agree. I'll call Maggie now and ask her to speak with dispatch. We are trying to keep information about the murders off the radio.

There are too many news people monitoring our calls. That reminds me, I need to deliver a news conference. Want to lend a hand? I don't want to share something I shouldn't."

"I will be glad to help prepare the news release. However, I won't be at the conference unless I can be invisible. My attendance would create more havoc than what you need right now. All that will change once the rest of my team arrives in town. Can you suggest a hotel close by? Five specialists from the FBI will come into town tomorrow if I can make it happen that quickly."

"We have one not too far from the sheriff's office. I'll make a call, and the manager will hold six rooms, then we can stop by the hotel once we finish at the Snappy Mart, and you can complete the registration."

"Sounds like a plan. Thanks for being so gracious. Sometimes we run into roadblocks with our kind if you know what I mean." Agent Ivey's cell phone dings with an incoming message. She immediately dials the phone. "Bud, it's Lana. What do you have for me?"

As I listen to the one-sided conversation, my heart rate quickens. It sounds as if the FBI has a possible ID on the sneaker owner. We are sitting in the car on the side of Shallow Bottoms Road, and I try to turn my attention to my surroundings. As I glance around, I see nothing of importance. There is a small unused pasture on one side of the road with missing fencing and a forest bordering the other side. No houses or farmland in sight, especially since the road is challenging to navigate in rough weather when moisture turns the red clay slick. Agent Ivey ends her call, and I wait patiently for an update.

"Sheriff, that was Bud, my partner. He reported a possible ID on one victim. We sent documents to the medical examiner's office in Tallahassee, Florida. The medical examiner will meet with the girl's parents and ask them to make an identification based on a photo of the body and the clothes she was wearing at the time of death. If it is a match, this girl was a cheerleader at a high school in Tallahassee. We should get the results within two hours. Let's make our way to the Snappy Mart. By the time we conclude our visit there, we should have our answer."

"Interesting. One girl might be from Tallahassee. The killer snatched the girl from Tallahassee and dumped her body in South Georgia. You stated earlier they found the other victims out of state. Wonder if that is a way to delay identification?" I ponder.

I check the mirrors before I travel from Shallow Bottoms Road to the main road. All kinds of thoughts fly through my brain. If I weren't driving, I would write notes in my notebook. What type of person can navigate through these many states in such a short time? Don't they have a job, or does their role allow them to drive all over the southeast United

States?

Sgt Taylor waits for us upon our arrival at the Snappy Mart. He carries his swagger well today. "Sgt Damon Taylor, this is FBI Agent Lana Ivey. Agent Ivey, this is Sgt Taylor. He is our lead investigator on the case."

"I don't mean to stare, but you drive a patrol car, and you are in uniform, yet you are the lead on the murder case." Agent Ivey inquires with a head tilt.

Sgt Taylor replies, "Yes. Our sheriff's department is a little different from most as we cross-train our deputies. The first deputy on the scene is the lead for that case, regardless of the crime. If a Rookie responds first, we tag team. It makes the job more interesting because each call is different in its own way. You can go from a lost child to murder in an eight-hour shift."

"That's a great idea. More departments should adapt your setup." Agent Ivey says as she looks over at me. "Was that your idea, Sheriff? Or has it always been like that?"

"Our office has always been on the smaller side since our population is lower compared to surrounding counties with our square mileage. In other words, we cover a lot of miles. We're just low on people, and that makes us low on money. Cross-training is the best use of the current workforce. We only hire the smartest applicants, so we can count on them to handle anything that comes along. My dad tried the patrol deputy and the investigator's department's style, but our budget afforded one investigator, and they sometimes took a vacation. At certain times of the year, we were short of workers, so I changed it when I took over. The department has been operating like this for the last few years. Sgt Taylor was my first hire."

Agent Ivey glows as I answer her question. She likes the way I run the sheriff's office. "Phenomenal. I've always enjoyed thinking outside of the box. Trying new things, you never know what might work. Sheriff and Sgt Taylor, show me around the Snappy Mart."

I point to Sgt Taylor and let him lead the way. We walk around the side of the mart towards the marked trail to show the sneaker's location. Sgt Taylor speaks first, "Agent Ivey, Roxy, Sal's dog, recovered the sneaker. Sal owns the Snappy Mart. He let Roxy out, and when she returned, she was carrying the sneaker. Deputy Tuttle stopped by the store right after the dog came in with it. Sal questioned Tuttle, Tuttle called Sheriff, and there you go."

"Is there anything out here, like a house, shed, barn? Anything that a person might use to get out of the weather?" Agent Ivey questions us as she glances around at her surroundings.

Sgt Taylor answers for us. "There are no buildings of any kind out here. That's why we thought it strange that Roxy found the sneaker. Here you go, Ivey. You are standing in the area where Rufus found the matching sneaker."

Agent Ivey turns her head towards us and says, "Rufus? I thought we were talking about Roxy."

I snicker a little, "Rufus is a tracking dog. Our budget at the sheriff's office doesn't allow enough funds to pay for a dog, but we have Deputy Johnson. He loves tracking dogs, so Rufus is family-owned, but we borrow him occasionally and help with costs when we can. Rufus has never let us down."

"Ah. I get it now. You had me confused with Rufus when Roxy found the shoe. Can I assume you walked all around the area with Rufus?"

"Yes, Agent Ivey, we did. Deputy Johnson used the grid method, and it comprised a wider arc than normal. We didn't want to miss anything. Rufus only alerted on the sneaker. There were no other traces of a crime," explained Sgt Taylor.

"I'm impressed Rufus found the other shoe. Wonder how and why the shoes are out here? It makes little sense." Agent Ivey states more to herself than anyone.

"We spotted a small portion of the box truck on the video surveillance from the Snappy Mart, but it is not enough to identify it. The truck parked at the curb, but Sal's camera points towards the gas pumps in case of drive-offs. There isn't another camera angle. However, Sal never got back to us with the name of the employee who worked that day. Maybe the worker remembered an out-of-town guy stopping in for something." I advise Ivey as we walk, and I think to myself to follow up with Sal.

"Sheriff, with a little luck, the employee might remember." Agent Ivey apparently always looks at the bright side.

We walk back to the Snappy Mart, and I motion my intent, "I'm going into the store and find out who worked the other day when the truck stopped here. You can come in too if you like, or you can wait outside. I'm sure Sgt Taylor wouldn't mind hanging with you until I finish."

Sgt Taylor straightens his back and responds, "you bet. I'll be glad to wait with Ivey."

As I enter the store, I glance back at the two of them standing by my car, and I give Agent Ivey a wink. She figures out that Sgt Taylor wants some alone time. I'm not sure how old she is, but she looks closer to Sgt Taylor's age than I. Who knows? They may fall madly in love if Agent Ivey can handle the swagger.

Sal stands behind the counter, helping a customer when I enter. He waves at me. "Hi, Sal, I was following up on our find the other day. Can you tell me who was working the counter the day the box truck parked at the curb? If the driver didn't get gas, maybe he came inside for something."

"Let me check the schedule, Sheriff. Louise or Joseph worked that night. I was working in the back. Give me a second." Sal strides off to his office in the back of the store.

As I wait for Sal to return, customers enter the store and stare at me. I usher them towards the counter and reassure them Sal will be back shortly. "Here you go, Sheriff. Louise was on duty. Her phone number is on the back of the card because she doesn't work until next week. Hope that helps." Sal passes the card to me as he walks behind the counter.

"Thanks, Sal. I really appreciate it. Maybe if he came inside, Louise could remember what the guy looks like." Exiting the store, I hope Louise can help us. When I turn the corner, Agent Ivey and Sgt Taylor are having a private conversation. So, they don't notice me approaching. How do I handle the intrusion? It's obvious they're enjoying each other's company.

Clearing my throat so I won't catch them off guard, I ask, "Are we ready to roll? Sal produced a name and a number for the employee working when the truck stopped. Hopefully, Louise can describe the driver. A description would help us find him. Ivey, we need to get you to the hotel to complete registration for your crew."

Sgt Taylor's shoulders droop when I mention leaving. So, I make him feel better when I say, "Ivey and I are eating supper after the hotel stop. If you aren't on a call, would you like to join us, Taylor?"

"Yes, I would. Thanks, Sheriff." Sgt Taylor answers as he blushes from the neck up.

As I get into my car, I turn my face away so no one can see me laugh. "Sheriff, is something funny?" Agent Ivey inquires.

"Yes, it is. I've never seen Sgt Taylor act this way before. It appears he has taken a liking to you, Ivey." I notice her expression, and her eyes say it all.

We pull out of the Snappy Mart parking lot and head for the hotel. I call Maggie to make sure things are running smoothly, and she says the only calls today were from the media. Maggie rambles on for a while, and finally, I end the call.

"After the hotel and food, I must sit down long enough to take care of the press conference." Glancing at Agent Ivey while I drive, I add, "If you can pass along some pointers, I would be grateful. Like I said before, I don't want to say the wrong thing and incite panic in the county. Although there isn't much to say since the evidence is scarce."

"My suggestion is to state facts only, including the crime scene location, sneakers, and the box truck. There are no suspects yet. If they ask about the FBI, of course, you say yes. Don't identify us by name. We don't want to get caught up in the media yet. It might happen later if the killer is from around here, but we would like to stay under the radar until then. Don't admit we have identified a body—give her parents time to pick up the body and get back home. They don't need the media swooping in for face-to-face interviews right now. Unfortunately, for them, that time will come soon enough."

"Sounds like a plan I can handle. If you haven't noticed, I've only had a handful of press releases and nothing about a serial killer. Thanks for the help. Would you be willing to read the release? The news conference will be tomorrow afternoon at 1:00."

"Absolutely. I wouldn't mind at all. Now, tell me about Sgt Taylor." Agent Ivey says with a sly expression on her face.

"So, you like him? The truth comes out. Well, it's obvious he is nice looking and single. I don't recall him dating much. He's dated no one for a long stretch that I can remember. After we eat dinner and you read the press release, I'll leave you two alone."

"I'm not sure, Sheriff. I didn't travel to Georgia in search of a love interest. My job is to catch a killer. But I feel like I've known Sgt Taylor forever." Ivey confesses.

"Ivey, a decent man doesn't pop into your life every day. What's the harm in spending a little time with Sgt Taylor and go from there? It's not like you live here. You both know the FBI will call you away for another case."

As I pull out of the space, I glance at

Agent Ivey. She is in deep concentration, I assume, over Sgt Taylor. I feel for her. Being a woman in a man's job is hard enough, but when a roadblock comes along and you want to take a detour, it becomes more challenging. Agent Ivey is attractive with no need for makeup. She is tall with long brunette hair, which she wears in a ponytail. Ivey is one of the lucky ones, as it takes nothing for her to be pretty. She wears the typical FBI attire, black pants, a white shirt, and a black jacket. Since I know Sgt Taylor, I think it will do him good to have a lady in his life, even if it is for only a few days.

Arriving at the hotel, we meet the manager and take care of the FBI's rooms. Her FBI staff already handled most of the details, making check-in easier than expected. As we leave the manager's office, my cell phone signals a text message. After clicking it open, I grin.

"What's so funny, Sheriff?" Agent Ivey asks.

"Sgt Taylor saved a table for us at the restaurant next door. I would say he is overly anxious. Just to forewarn you, as soon as I eat, I will excuse myself. Sgt Taylor can bring you back to the hotel. I'll handle his calls tonight for a little while."

"Sheriff, I can't ask you to do that. You must be exhausted."

"You didn't ask. I want to do it. It makes me happy to see people I like happy. Today has been slow for us. Take the time while you can. Things can change in an instant as we know." I remind her.

Agent Ivey pauses before she answers, "You are right. I guess I needed a reminder of that fact. I'll take you up on your offer. Wish me luck."

"You don't need that. I think it depends on what you want. Enjoy your time." I state.

Our trip to the restaurant is silent. We are both lost in our thoughts. The parking lot is busier than usual. So much for a quick dinner. My brain is sorting out the press release and still hanging on to the hope that Louise saw the guy with the truck, and my brain can only hold so much information. My notebook helps with capacity issues.

Sgt Taylor stands when he sees us enter the building. As we walk towards him, I realize we are sitting in a booth. I don't question the seating arrangements. I slide in on the bench opposite Sgt Taylor and Agent Ivey, I wink at Sgt Taylor, and he blushes.

Dinner is nice with small talk. However, I spend most of my time listening to the lovebirds get acquainted even though they try to include me in their conversation. I swallow my last bite of steak and leave for the office without mentioning the press conference.

Within an hour, the press release is complete. I take Agent Ivey's advice about stating facts. If the morning goes as planned, the press release should go off without a hitch. However, I would like confirmation from the medical examiner in Tallahassee before the press conference. That tidbit would add one more fact to my growing list. I hate to admit we don't have a suspect. With the press release written, I breathe a sigh of relief. Turning out the lights in my office, I notice how quiet it is. The deputies are on patrol or at home waiting for a call. At least I'm not too strict. With the deputies on night patrol, most of our county is asleep or working on a factory line, so letting them stay home on a slow night, helps with morale. But when dad was sheriff, they had to stay at the office if they weren't on patrol. He said the public likes to see patrol cars out in the county. Impressions are difference makers.

The radio squawks when I get into the car. I lifted the mic to my mouth and replied, "Sheriff Steele."

Chapter 5

More crackling noises and then the response sends shivers up my spine, "Sheriff, we received a report on our BOLO for the box truck. The caller mentioned the truck is traveling north on Route 33."

"Show me in route. Is Tuttle still on dinner break?"

"10-4. He is not due back for thirty minutes, Sheriff."

"10-4. I'll handle the report and call if I need help." I slid the mic back in its holder.

I flip the lights and sirens and make my way to Route 33. Traffic is moderate as I drive closer to Route 33. People are courteous in our county, which makes my drive short as I cruise north for miles. "Dispatch, this is Sheriff Steele. Did the caller say they were on Route 33 when they saw the truck?"

"Negative, Sheriff. The caller's phone connection was poor. Identification on the caller remains unknown."

"10-4. I'll continue to search and see if I pick up on anything."

Through my body, the adrenaline courses as I desperately want to find that truck and put the killer behind bars. Cruising the streets, I see no signs of a box truck. There are several cross streets off Route 33 that require checking. However, glancing down the side streets, they are almost empty, as most people are already home for the night.

"Sheriff, Tuttle here. What's your status?"

"Tuttle, crisscrossing Route 33 searching for the box truck and nothing so far. I will be here for a while longer. What's your status?"

"Coming your way. Meet me at Route 33 and Timberwood Road."

"10-4." I returned the mic to its holder as my eyes scanned the area.

One street before I meet Tuttle, I round the corner in an industrial area and spot a box truck parked on the side of the road next to a building. "Tuttle, Sheriff Steele. I'm requesting backup at Milton Trucking on the southeast side of the building. A box truck matching our description is in sight."

"10-4. In route." As Tuttle completes the call, I hear the sirens. He will be at my location in two minutes. There is no movement anywhere. The inside of the building appears dark. However, something activated a security light at the other end of the lot when I entered. So, is someone standing in the lot staring at me? I can't remember the last time I pulled my service weapon from its holster, but I do tonight.

Deputy Tuttle makes it to my location in under two minutes. He did well as he pulled in behind my car at an angle. Tuttle exits his vehicle and walks my way. Glancing down at my weapon, he knows we are in an

55

unpredictable situation, and I take no chances. "What's up, Sheriff?"

"See the security light at the end of the building? Why is it shining? The light turned on as I pulled into the lot. Why? Can you see anyone down there, or did you pass a vehicle on your way into the lot?"

Thinking about my explanation, Tuttle shakes his head from side to side, then pulls his service weapon. "Better safe than sorry when you put it that way. Are we checking out the truck?" Tuttle points at it.

"Yes, I'll take the driver's side. You take the passenger side. If the cab is empty, we will go back to the box and open it up." Deputy Tuttle doesn't bother with a reply. He walks off, and I jog to catch up.

As we inch our way down the truck towards the cab, I notice nothing unusual. The truck is clean, whereas our witness's description stated the truck was dirty, but this truck is vacant of markings too. We make it to the cab with both of us leading gun first. The cab of the truck is empty except for a few scraps of papers, maybe loading receipts. After we scour the truck for information on the owner, we open the back, and it is empty. There are pallet-sized markings on the floor, proving the truck once stored something. The truck is empty. I still can't explain the security light illuminating the back lot.

"Tuttle, I will call the owner of this

business in the morning and get information on the truck. I have the VIN too. Thanks for watching my six."

"Anytime, Sheriff. I'm heading back to the office. What about you?"

"I'm going home. If you need me, call."

As I approach my car, I listen to my radio calling my name. "Steele, here. Come back."

"Sheriff, it's Taylor and Ivey. What's your status? When the call came in, we couldn't raise either of you on the radio. We are in route to your location."

"Turn around. Both of us are fine. I am heading home, and Tuttle is returning to the office. Thanks for checking. The truck somewhat fits the description. I'll follow up with the owner in the morning." I stated.

Sgt Taylor responds 10-4 with apprehension in his voice. He always worries about my safety. He is a protector, and he makes a fine one. I can only hope Agent Ivey and Sgt Taylor become good friends. At least something good will have come from all the violence.

I spend the rest of the night in a restless sleep. Images of the dead girls appear in my dreams, then a car chase, and another search for the truck. When my alarm clock blares, I want to crawl under the covers and stay there. I feel like I ran a marathon overnight. Too much time has elapsed between the discovery of the bodies and now. One girl's identification is the only lead. Remembering the girl's family should be in town this morning, I jump up, shower, dress, and run to the car. I want to be in the office when they arrive.

With the sun shining in my face, I feel better about today. The press release is ready for one o'clock today. That was one worry off my list for the day. As I drive around the office to the back lot, I notice a car with Florida tags. Wonder if the car belongs to the victim's family?

The office is busy. TV people are in the lobby waiting to see me. I advise them of the press conference later in the day. It doesn't take long for them to clear out, which turns out to be perfect timing. The medical examiner enters the department through the back door, and I quickly usher him into my office, where Tina's parents are waiting. I laid a picture of a deceased girl on my desk, and they identify her as their daughter, a high school cheerleader, only sixteen years old. The shoes belonged to her. Tina's parents noticed the other two pictures and asked about them.

"These girls were found with Tina." I offered in a low voice.

"So, other Florida families are missing their daughters too." Tina's mom whispered.

With this information, I immediately text Agent Ivey and then ask Tina's parents, "You stated other families from Florida are missing their daughters too. How do you know they are from Florida? Would you have the other parent's contact information?"

Tina's parents shake their heads. They assumed the girls were from Florida too. Tina's dad gave us someone to contact at the Tallahassee Police Department. Agent Ivey could deal with the detective in Florida. Indeed, she would carry more clout than a South Georgia Sheriff.

Sitting at my desk, I watch Tina's parents leave. The pain of losing a child is apparent in their faces and their body language. With heads bowed and shoulders slumped, they exit the door. No one recovers from an event such as a child's death.

Two minutes later, Agent Ivey walks in with a strange expression on her face. "They identified another girl as Lucy Monroe. She was also a cheerleader from the same area, age sixteen, but they have received nothing on the last victim yet. The detective will call me back."

"Interesting. Two cheerleaders from the same area. Is the killer cruising the area and somehow snatching girls from different schools? Where is he keeping them? Something is amiss. Do sixteen-year-old girls get into a stranger's vehicle? That's what younger kids do, right?"

Agent Ivey runs through some ideas before she states, "Yes, you are correct. Maybe the girls knew each other through cheerleading." Agent Ivey walks to the board and scribbles

59

something I can't read.

"Whoa, Ivey, what does that say? Didn't you learn penmanship in school?" I ask her jokingly, but apparently, I upset her with the outburst. When I look up, she is pouting. "What's wrong? I didn't mean for that to come out as it did. My apologies."

"I've heard it all my life. My mom always made negative comments about my handwriting. She says it reminds her of a doctor's signature. I took penmanship in school, but somehow it didn't help. I wrote cheerleading on the board."

My brain is working overtime. I've seen writing like that before, but the ringing phone on my desk breaks my concentration. I answer and listen patiently as Doc James explains they might have identification for all three girls by the end of the day. After the call ends, I pose a question to Agent Ivey.

"Doc James told me the identification of all three girls might be available by the end of the day. Should I include their names in the press release? My gut tells me to ignore the press and let the parents get back home with their daughters first. Maybe release the names in 48 hours or so."

"I like the way you think, Sheriff. Go with your gut." Agent Ivey turns and leaves me alone with my thoughts. I add several items to the board. As the marker hits the tabletop, my cell phone rings.

"Sheriff, this is Deputy Johnson. A call came into dispatch regarding a missing fifteen-year-old girl from the county high school. Want to meet there?"

"Absolutely. No radio traffic. Ivey will come along. Meet us in the parking lot at the front entrance."

My insides twisted as the call ends. Then the hair on my neck stood up as I pondered the situation. I don't like the sound of this—a missing high-schooler right here in my county. There are no coincidences. I call Deputy Johnson back, "Johnson, bring Rufus to the school."

"He's in the back, ready for work." Rufus lets out several loud barks.

"At least he sounds happy. See you soon."

Agent Ivey has disappeared. No reply to texts or calls. As I'm walking towards the ladies' room, she comes out. "Are you okay, Ivey? I've been looking for you. There is a missing high school girl right here in our county. We need to roll."

"Let's go, then. I'll grab my things on the way out the door."

I watch as Ivey goes into my office for her bag and realize her face is a little pale. "Did you enjoy a late-night last night?"

"That would be affirmative, Sheriff. Sgt Taylor and I had a good time after we found out you and Tuttle were okay. We talked into the wee hours of the morning. Once I made it back to the hotel, I couldn't sleep. I had too many thoughts about him and the case."

"I understand. We will finish that topic of conversation later. Deputy Eli Johnson and Rufus are meeting us at the high school, and the principal is waiting in his office."

The school sits in the middle of the county on a beautiful piece of property. A heavily wooded parcel borders it to the rear, and it's wide open on the other three sides. The football field sits parallel to the school building, while the baseball field is off to the left. There is no fencing around the school, so anyone can come and go as they please. However, no one can enter the school building without checking in at the front desk. They lock the doors from the inside, but I carry a key, as do the local fire department members.

Agent Ivey takes in the scene as we enter the school grounds. "The school is gorgeous. Is it the only high school in the county?"

"Yes. The county has one high school, one elementary, and one middle school. While the elementary school is overcrowded, they make do with their space. We don't have enough children to build another school yet. However, with our population inching up over the past several years, we will have to build schools soon to accommodate the expected growth. Come on. I want to get a jump on this situation."

We exit the car and enter the school's front door, and I wave to the front desk ladies on the way to the principal's office. He is on the phone when we enter, and he motions us to a chair. Since my nerves are working overtime, I stand next to the door. Agent Ivey takes the chair. I can't tell who he was speaking with, but it doesn't last long.

"Sheriff, thanks for coming so fast." Mr. Hale states. Then he continues, "What a nightmare! Tonya Zon, the missing girl, was last seen in the third period. I confirmed her homeroom attendance based on roll call. Her best friend reported her missing to her science teacher."

"This is FBI Agent Ivey, Mr. Hale. Don't jump to conclusions. Agent Ivey was already in town working with us on the three bodies found on Shallow Bottoms Road. She came along to help. Can we speak with Tonya's friend?" I explain Agent Ivey's presence, hoping to deter alarm. But we watch as Mr. Hale's eyes grow big.

"Sure, Sheriff. She is waiting in the teacher's lounge. Her name is Darlene, and she is distraught. So, I'm not sure how much help she will be."

Her condition is understandable. However, if Darlene was the last one to see Tonya, she can describe her clothing. We walk to the teacher's lounge to find Darlene staring out the window. "Hi, Darlene. I'm Sheriff

Steele, and this is Agent Ivey. We have a few questions about Tonya. Can you help us?"

Darlene sniffs and wipes her eyes with a tissue. "I'll try." She twists her body to face us.

The questions start, and I try to be gentle, but time is of the essence. "What was Tonya wearing today?"

"She was wearing blue jeans with an untucked, plaid button-down shirt. That shirt was her favorite. She was wearing black ankle booties with a tassel on the side."

"Good. You've provided usable information, Darlene. Is there any reason Tonya would leave school without telling someone? She isn't answering her cell phone nor her home phone, so we don't think she went home."

Darlene thinks back over the morning and then replies, "Tonya didn't act upset this morning. She seemed happy but a little anxious. Usually, Tonya is talkative during homeroom, but she kept looking at her phone like she was waiting for a call or text from someone."

I continue with another question, "Does Tonya have a boyfriend?"

"Not a steady boyfriend. She is homecoming queen, and many of the guys try to date her, but her emphasis is on her college grades. Tonya's goal is to be the face in makeup ads and stuff and then move to Hollywood." Darlene looks down at her hands and fiddles with the tissue she still holds.

"Oh, wow. That's a huge goal. Are

Tonya's books still in her locker? And one last question, is there anything going on at home that would make her want to run away?" Darlene's answer is instant, "Tonya's family is great. They get along and everything. I haven't checked her locker. You will find Tonya, won't you?" Darlene's eyes filled with tears as she waits for an answer.

"We will do everything possible to find Tonya and bring her home. Thanks for your help, Darlene. You can go back to class now." Darlene walks through the door and down the hallway with her head and shoulders down, showing signs of uncontrollable sobs.

Agent Ivey stands and walks over to the door, "Let's get Mr. Hale to check Tonya's locker, but I bet her things are still there."

We meet Mr. Hale in the hallway and explain what we need. He leads the way to the bank of lockers. Mr. Hale cuts the lock off of her locker for us. Unfortunately, Agent Ivey is correct. Tonya's things are still in her locker, and that proves Tonya had no intention of leaving for good. The good news for us, Rufus has a recent article of clothing belonging to Tonya. "I will borrow her sweatshirt, Mr. Hale. Rufus is in the parking lot, waiting to go to work."

"Absolutely, Sheriff. I'll be in my office if you need anything." Mr. Hale turns around and wanders off.

Rufus is outside, waiting in the grass

with his head high and his tongue hanging out the side of his mouth. Rufus knows how to work, and he's ready. Deputy Johnson speaks, "We are ready, Sheriff. Which direction?"

"I'm guessing, but the woods would be my first choice. Here is Tonya's sweatshirt. Let Rufus sniff the scent. Tonya had to leave from the front door or the side door closest to the road." I gave the shirt to Deputy Johnson.

"Tonya? Tonya Zon is missing?" Deputy Johnson's eyes grow big.

"Yes, do you know her?"

"Unbelievable. Yes. Tonya's dad owns the hardware store out on 33, and since I have been working on my house, he gave me some pointers on carpentry work. Taylor introduced him to me. Have they notified her dad yet?"

Agent Ivey and I look at each other before answering, "Not sure. Mr. Hale didn't share if he has notified the family or not. I would hope he has by now. Let's get started."

Rufus does his thing. He sniffs, drinks water, and sniffs again. Finally, he is ready. Deputy Johnson tugs on his leash, and Rufus is in work mode. He picks up Tonya's scent at the edge of the road then enters the woods, nose to the ground. Every so often, Rufus lifts his head, looks around, then his nose goes back to the ground and takes off running. He has fantastic sniffing abilities. It is fascinating to watch. You always wonder what he will find.

Chapter 6

We run some and walk some through the
woods, but Rufus doesn't find Tonya. A few
times, Rufus acts like he's caught the scent, but
nothing pans out. Deputy Johnson stops Rufus
and readdresses the smell. The wood's part on
the backside, and we walk out onto a one-lane
dirt road. "This must be a fire road or
something. I don't remember this road being
here. What's the road's name, Johnson?" I ask
as I survey my new surroundings.

"This road is unfamiliar to me too. It's
not on maps apps either, based on my phone.
Here are small tire tracks, like an ATV. I'll walk
Rufus up the road a little way and see if we find
anything. Why don't you two walk the other
way, and we will meet back here in a few
minutes? Call me if you find anything." Deputy
Johnson suggests.

The road is a narrow, winding dirt road.
Someone still uses it, but who and why? I've
been in this county forever, and I remember
nothing about it. The property tax office will
have the owner's information. This is so odd, a
dirt road in the middle of the woods. Maybe it is
a fire road used by the Department of Natural
Resources. I thought my dad had taken me on
every road in the county, but not this one.

As I glance back, I can barely see

Deputy Johnson since we are so far apart. I can't believe we did not recover a single trace of evidence. We have nothing. Who is drawing these girls out, and how? The answer to that question will be our way of catching this guy.

"Ivey, here's a question. How are these victims related, and what is it that draws them out to meet with an unknown person?"

"I'm working on a scenario. The victims are high-school age, so they are not susceptible to something like a missing dog or candy. The victims are expecting something from this person, or they wouldn't attempt to meet. My question is: what does the guy promise these girls?"

"The victims were pretty, cheerleaders, blonde, or brunette hair." As I finish my statement, my cell phone rings, and I speak with Deputy Johnson. He asks us to turn around and head back. They found nothing on their walk. Rufus failed to catch Tonya's scent, and now they are heading back to the place we left him. After the call, I share this with Ivey.

"Johnson instructs us to head back. They didn't find anything either." There is a little breeze in the trees now, making the walk more bearable. On the way back to Johnson, I glance on both sides of the road, but you can only see so far into the woods. It is dark in there, with the treetops creating canopies across the forest floor.

"The breeze is pleasant," Agent Ivey

says, almost as if she just read my mind. "The outdoors are fun, but I got little of it growing up in Louisiana. The bugs are so big, and mom didn't allow me to play outside in the evenings often. So, I spent a lot of time playing volleyball in the gym at school."

"I love the outdoors too. Dad taught me how to fish, and I learned to swim in the lake. I played basketball throughout high school and spent many hours inside a hot and stuffy gym, too." As I described my childhood, Agent Ivey and I look at each other. We are friends now. Each of us has shared something personal. I'm usually not like that—I don't share personal stuff with anyone. Dad was the only one I talked to about personal things. Since he died, I have had no one to share my thoughts with, except Maggie.

As we meet up with them, Deputy Johnson tugs on Rufus's leash to slow him. Typically, Rufus is very docile when he is not working. With the wind blowing, Rufus has caught a whiff of something. With his lead extended, Rufus bounds over to the side of the road and alerts.

Tucked into a briar bush is a swatch of plaid fabric that matches Tonya's shirt. Deputy Johnson takes photos of the material, then bags and tags it. He marks the area with spray paint. "I will call for more deputies, Sheriff. There is still time to search the woods with at least three more hours of daylight."

"Great idea. Ivey and I will head back to the office. I want to have a brainstorming session, and I also need to call Louise. There is a key to this mess somewhere, and someone holds it. Call my cell phone with any information. Oh, and Johnson, give that dog a bone!"

"Will do. I'll call for Tuttle and Taylor." Deputy Johnson leads Rufus to the car to make calls, and we walk back to my vehicle. Since we don't have an update, I don't stop by the school again. We have zip, other than a piece of cloth. The odds of the guys finding anything else in the woods are slim to none, too.

The drive to the sheriff's office is uneventful with another round of small talk. We are both lost in our thoughts when Agent Ivey's cell phone rings. She talks for a few minutes, then turns and says, "Bud and the crew are here. Would you mind taking me to the hotel? I want you to meet them."

"Absolutely." After replying, I call Maggie to give her a quick update on the search for Tonya Zon. The media are already calling. Maggie says she's already placed stacks of messages on my desk, all requesting an update. At the end of the conversation, I advise her that I will be with Agent Ivey at the hotel to meet the FBI crew.

The hotel staff offered the FBI agents the use of a conference room while they are in town. The FBI Team set the room up like an office, with whiteboards along the walls and laptops scattered around the room. As we entered the room, all eyes turn to us. Agent Ivey introduces me to her peers. Bud, her partner, walks over and shakes my hand. He holds onto it a little longer than I expected. At least, that's the way I feel. I don't dare look at Agent Ivey. I don't want to give her a reason to tease me. Now, I know why she brought me here.

While I stand off to the side, Agent Ivey brings Bud up to speed on the latest missing girl. Every so often, I notice Bud looking at me. I try not to stare, but it is hard. He is taller than me by several inches, with an athletic build, dark, wavy hair with some graying at the temples, broad shoulders, and a thick neck. He might have been a football player during his school years, just like Taylor. Now, my words to Agent Ivey about men come back to bite me.

A cell phone rings, and it takes a minute for me to realize it is mine. I must focus on my task, and Bud is not my task. As I answer the phone, Doc James speaks. With my notebook in hand, I jot down the information. Angelina Cortez is our third victim. She was also a high school cheerleader but attended a different school than our first two girls. They located no cell phone or purse, just like the other victims. After he finishes, I thank him for the call.

Once the call from Doc James ends, I consider the information. Is it possible that the killer has possession of the victims' cell phones and purses? Are these items trophies from the kills, or is the killer disposing of them? If we can somehow get social media information on these girls, we might get a lead. Wonder if they posted anything about meeting someone new? FBI should be able to help with getting warrants for social media accounts.

"Ivey, have a minute?" I finish my thoughts on this angle and decide I want to share it with her and ask for help.

"Sure, Sheriff. What's up?"

"Doc James called and provided the identification for our third girl. Angelina Cortez was also a high school cheerleader, but she attended a different school than the first two girls. Her cell phone and purse were also missing. How hard would it be to get a warrant to search the victims' social media accounts? I want to see if they posted anything about meeting someone new."

"That's not too difficult, but it takes time. We can use a friend's account like Darlene to dig into Tonya. Darlene might let us view her personal page, then Tonya's page would be visible from there. As far as the other three victims, that might be a little difficult since they were from Tallahassee, and we don't have access to their friends. However, Bud can process the warrants for those."

I meander over to a table at the end of the room and call Deputy Johnson. "How's it going, Johnson? Did you find anything useful?"

He describes his ordeal in detail. They spent two more hours in the woods, and Rufus found zip. Deputy Johnson explains his hunch on Tonya. He thinks someone forced her into a vehicle in the area where Rufus located a scrap of material. There would be no other reason for the fabric to be there. That idea rolls around in my head. "You might be right. Can you let the guys know we will meet at the office at 9:00 am? It will be a brief update."

When I raise my eyes, Bud is standing in front of me. "Hi, Sheriff Steele. Ivey told me a lot about you. I'm glad to put a face to the name finally. I just want to make you aware the warrants are in the works. Maybe we can have dinner one night while we are in town."

"Thanks for the warrants, and dinner sounds good." I look around for Agent Ivey and wave at her. Bud doesn't leave, so I add, "I need to get back to the office. The media are climbing the walls looking for an update on Tonya."

"We'll talk later, and I'll let Ivey know you are going to the office," Bud offers.

Quickly, I leave Bud standing at the door. I'm not sure why talking with men is so difficult. Maybe I am in the middle of a critical investigation, and I don't need or want the complication that a relationship would bring. Agent Ivey has already shared her concerns after meeting Sgt Taylor. I certainly don't want to insert myself into the same situation.

As I return to the office, I see that the

TV reporters have made themselves at home in the lobby. I swallow hard when I see what has happened in my absence. They now occupy every lobby chair, and while some even sit on the floor leaning against the wall. Usually, I'm not one to lose my cool, but at present, I lost it.

"Ladies and gentlemen, you are in a sheriff's office, not a hotel. Please gather your things and vacate the premises within ten minutes. This is a final warning. The sheriff's department will notify you of a press release. If you are still here in ten minutes, we will arrest and book you accordingly." Glancing around the room, people pack their things, and some run out the front door for fear of being arrested. Who will test me? One will—it's inevitable—and I am ready for it.

My office is dark, but the mound of phone messages on top of my desk seems to glow. I am too tired to count the number of pink slips. As I thumb the stack, I see all but a handful are from the media. Some names are recognizable from big TV shows. I sit and stare at contacts for Good Morning America and several news stations in Atlanta. The most important message is a call from Louise. I sink a little deeper in my chair. What is happening to my county? Am I losing control? Why did the killer choose my county?

After I separate the messages into stacks, local and away, I work my way through them, but Louise is first, so I call her. Then I call the rest and repeat the same statements until I return all messages. The whiteboard in my office glares back at me, so I update it with what recent information Louise provided and what I remember without the use of my notes since my notebook lies on the front passenger seat of my car. After the update, the whiteboard is full of information, and I draw lines connecting people and places. An interesting map is evolving. It shows that two of the dead girls attended the same school in Tallahassee. The third girl attended another school—no correlation to the other girls. The only connection is cheerleading, which seems to be the link to Tonya.

Unfortunately, Louise wasn't a lot of help. She remembers a stranger coming into the store for only snacks. The guy wore a baseball cap, pulled low on his forehead, with jeans and a plain white t-shirt. She had a hard time describing height and weight, so we are back to zero. That guy could have been any one of a thousand in this county.

Every school has cheerleading coaches, so that seems a good starting place. I pluck my cell phone from my pocket and call Mr. Hale. "Hi. Mr. Hale, this is Sheriff Steele. I'd like to speak to your cheerleading coach. The deceased girls, along with Tonya, were all cheerleaders. Since I've never been one, I'd like to see how it works. Can you ask the coach to call me?

"Coach Turner is with students now, but the class ends in thirty minutes. I'll have her call then." Mr. Hale answers hurriedly.

"Is something wrong, sir? It sounds as if you are in a hurry."

"Yes, Sheriff, we are preparing for a pep rally for our ballgame tonight. We are continuing with our studies and recreation, but with Tonya still missing, it's hard." Mr. Hale explains.

"That is completely understandable. We are diligently searching for her. Thanks for having Coach Turner call." I end the call as my heart sinks. I fear Tonya will not return to school.

A missing child is torturous, especially when the child disappears from school. School is some place you should feel comfortable letting your child attend. Children are there for months during the year. Mr. Hale has probably spent endless hours answering questions between the faculty, Tonya's parents, and the public. My job is hard enough, but I don't envy Mr. Hale.

I am leaning against my desk, staring at the whiteboard, when I feel a presence. Someone is standing in the doorway of my office. "Hi, Sheriff. I hope I'm not interrupting."

"Hi, Bud. Actually, I'm thankful for the interruption. The more I stare at it, the less I see it, if that makes sense. What can I do for you?" I ask as a flutter reaches my stomach.

"Personal delivery. I'm holding the warrants for the social media accounts for all the

Tallahassee girls. Did Darlene call about Tonya's social media accounts?" Bud enters my office and stands next to me.

"Mr. Hale, the school principal, advised the school is having a pep rally later today for a ballgame. I will call Darlene after that. Also, I've asked Mr. Hale to pass a phone message to Coach Turner to call me. She is the cheerleading coach. I have a few questions for Coach Turner too. Did Ivey ride with you?"

"No, Ivey is waiting on Taylor. They are holding seats for dinner if you are up for it. I don't want you to think I am this forward all the time because I'm not. Agent Ivey suggested I pick you up. She said you wouldn't eat if you were alone." Bud explained his actions with an eyebrow raised.

"Ivey is correct on that. I suppose it wouldn't hurt to eat, so let's join them."

"That was easier than I thought. Ivey said to brace up for war. I'm glad she was wrong." Bud grins, takes my elbow, and leads me out the door. It is odd having someone guide me. Usually, I'm the lead.

The rest of the day, including the evening, ends well. I haven't enjoyed a night out with friends in a long time. We all shared childhood stories and dreams. Sharing came easily with this group. Bud drives me back to the sheriff's office after dinner and walks me inside. We face the whiteboard, willing something to jump out at us.

After a few minutes pass, Bud looks over at me, "Sheriff, thank you for tonight. It was a pleasure spending time with you, and I hope we can do it again."

"I enjoyed it too, Bud, and I'm glad Ivey forced you to pick me up for dinner." I chuckle, thinking about how Bud persuaded me to join them for dinner.

Bud glances back at the board, "If you think cheerleading is the connection, how does someone from out of town contact victims?"

"You remember the warrants I requested for social media accounts? That's how I think the killer is contacting these girls. I'm just not sure which platform the killer uses because the victims were from multiple states. Social media is not my strongest subject."

"Mine either. Younger people are true users of social media because they know all the ins and outs. Our crew has a guy familiar with all of that. He will be in the hotel conference room in the morning. Want to meet for breakfast at the hotel? Then we can speak to him."

"Sure, around 8?" I ask, using the case as a reason to see more of Bud.

"Great. See you then. I'll show myself out." He pats me on the arm before leaving.

Here I sit in my office late into the night, pondering this case. I pull out my old road map. I wonder if a road or two connects my county to Tallahassee, Florida. If so, it would be a winding country road. With Tonya missing, where would the kidnappers take her? My cell phone rings deep in my pocket.

I answer without checking my caller ID. "Thanks for calling, Coach Turner. It's late, so I'll be brief. I'm not familiar with the inner workings of a cheerleading team. What can you tell me about cheerleading? Was Tonya a standout? How do the girls interact with one another? Anything you can tell will help."

"Cheerleading is an extremely competitive sport. Our competition squads attend meets and compete against local schools, then move up to state groups, and if you win state, you proceed to the district level. The district level is multi-state. Our county has competed with a few southeastern states over the years. Our school is excellent, and Tonya is one of the best. She is always willing to help the younger girls in their development."

"Do the cheerleaders communicate using social media just for cheerleaders, like closed groups or something? We are looking into different areas for clues that connect the victims. Cheerleading seems to be a good fit. Did you notice Tonya acting strangely the last time you saw her?"

"No, Sheriff. Tonya stayed late with me, helping one of our freshman girls. Tonya's mom picked her up right outside the gym. We all left at the same time. Tonya was smiling like always. I understand there is a social media group some cheerleaders use, but I'm not on it, so I can't help with that. I don't understand why someone would want to harm her." Coach Turner sniffs as she makes her statement.

"I wish I could answer. We have all-hands-on-deck searching for her. Thanks, Coach, for your time. You've given me something to think about. One more thing, would you have a list of past competitions your team attended over the last year?"

"If I do, it will be on my computer at school. I can check first thing in the morning. If it's there, I'll email it to you."

"Thanks again, Coach. I appreciate your time."

After the call, I lean back in my chair and close my eyes. Are these murders associated with cheerleading competitions? I would like to attend a tournament and see what happens at one. A guess would be a lot of young girls do routines for a group of judges. If the girls are not taking part, what do they do in their downtime? It sounds as if there would be a decent amount of free time in between the routines.

Updating the board takes more time than I realize. The clock strikes eleven, and I can't believe it. Breakfast will come soon if I don't get to bed. There is so much to think about in this case. So many states involved and so many girls. I make notes to ask Ivey and Bud about the cheerleading competition angle. Once that task is complete, I head home for some much-needed rest.

With my notebook tucked under my arm, I enter the hotel at eight for breakfast. Ivey and Bud are sitting in a booth with Taylor. Of course, the spot next to Bud is open. Bud stands and lets me slide in.

Everyone is drinking coffee and talking casually, and here I thought we would discuss the case. Cheerleading competition is still my bet on finding the killer. A cell phone rings, and all heads look at their own as I answer mine. I listen to the caller and advise him I will meet him at the store in twenty minutes. "Sorry, I'm being called away. Sal, from the Snappy Mart, has someone he wants me to see. Remember the ATV tracks we saw in the woods? He says the guy might have seen our ATV driver."

Ivey jumps in, "I'm going with you. So far, Sal has been right in the mix with news."

I bid farewell to Bud and Taylor and skip breakfast. With Ivey by my side, we jump into my car and hit the road. We bounce ideas around on our ride, but nothing sticks.

We pull into Sal's parking lot at the eighteen-minute mark. Sal is standing outside on the curb, talking with an older guy as he stands beside a bread truck. "Hey, Sal. What do you have for me?"

"Sheriff, this is Charlie. He delivers my bread weekly and has for years. You need to hear what he saw on his last delivery here. Go ahead, Charlie. Tell her." Sal looks at Charlie and nods his head my way.

"Sure, Sal. As I was unloading the bread, an engine revved, and when I looked up, there was an older model ATV racing along the road. And the driver crossed the street and went into the woods over there. A guy drove with a girl on the back. She was holding on for dear life, and by her expression, she was terrified."

"Can you show us where they entered the woods? Also, can you describe the ATV?"

"I can give you a general area. There isn't a road where they entered. The ATV was an older black and red model. For the driver's description, I can't say. I couldn't get the girl's facial expression out of my head. That's why I mentioned it to Sal."

Agent Ivey spoke up, "is there anything else you can remember?"

Charlie shook his head as he stated, "No, I don't think so. The more I thought about it, the more it bothered me. Oh, there was one more thing I felt was odd. The girl wasn't wearing shoes."

Chapter 7

We swallow hard as Charlie's words mean more to us than he will ever know. I glance at Ivey, and we both know our next stop. Charlie gives us his contact information in case we need him later. Wonder where we would be if Charlie offered this information when he saw them?

I call for Taylor, Johnson, and Rufus and update Maggie on the case from the car. She can keep the press away. Charlie gave us a general location of the ATV, so we park at the proposed spot on the road and wait for the others to arrive. Since we have time, I mention cheerleading competitions as a common denominator between bodies.

Ivey ponders the idea and eventually agrees. It is a viable lead. With Bud on the phone, we discuss my opinion. Bud will verify if the other girls were also in competition cheerleading squads. If so, our focus on the case will change.

The guys pull in behind us and exit their vehicles. Rufus is barking, which proves he is ready for another challenge. Gathered in between our cars, I update the guys on Charlie's information. Deputy Taylor pulls out his cell and uses the maps app. My deputies stay abreast of new technology since we depend on it more and more. "The app doesn't show a road, but that doesn't mean there isn't one there. It very well might be another fire road in there."

"Johnson, get Rufus ready. We are staying together while searching. The terrain on this side of the road is unfamiliar." As I finish speaking, everyone shakes their heads in agreement. "Let's get started."

Tall grasses sway in the slight breeze as we walk into the brush. The group searches for signs of an ATV or shoe prints. Rufus leads us deeper into the woods. His nose is to the ground, but he isn't running like he usually does. I question Johnson, "Hey, Johnson. Why is Rufus acting strange today?"

"Tonya's shirt gave him a scent, but with the wind blowing, it is hard to follow the scent because things move in the air. He puts his nose down, then raises it to compare before running again. When the wind blows, scents are hard to track. However, my concern is Tonya's shirt is losing her scent. It's not nearly as strong as it was during the first search."

We continue following Rufus and Johnson into the woods. The deeper we walk, the cooler the air. There are a few items of interest we mark for later. However, we find no tire tracks or footprints. It is eerily quiet in the woods when a noise sounds. Rufus alerts on it too. The sound comes from our left, and we walk alongside whatever makes the noise.

Johnson hangs back with Rufus while the rest of us walk toward the sound. I can't judge by my surroundings how deep into the woods we are, but whatever and whoever is making the noise, they probably thought no one would hear.

Taylor and I walk side by side with Ivey behind us. We creep towards the edge of the woods and find some guy trying to start an old ATV. There doesn't appear to be anyone else around, but I still felt apprehensive approaching him. I glance at Taylor and motion him to go left, and I will go right. Taylor points left for Ivey. He wants her with him, and I can't blame him either. Once we are in position, I motion to begin the approach.

We draw our guns as we advance, "Sheriff's Department! Hands in the air, knees on the ground, now!" Taylor shouts at the man.

"What is this?" The man asks as he turns around, startled by the command.

"Get on the ground! Now!" Taylor reaffirms the message, and this time, the man complies.

Taylor questions the man first, "What is your name? Show me some ID." The older man fumbled in his pants pocket for his wallet. He brings it out with shaky hands. Taylor reads it then asks, "You're John Smith?"

"I swear. That's what my mama named me. Been John Smith all my life."

I step forward. "John, I'm Sheriff Steele. Who owns the ATV you are hotwiring?"

"It's mine. I reported it missing to your office about a week ago. Once before, kids stole it for joyriding in these woods. I thought I would look for myself and save everyone some time and trouble." John explains.

"Where do you live, John?" Ivey jumps in on the conversation.

"Take the next left after you pass the Snappy Mart going out towards Shallow Bottoms Road."

"Did you see anyone unfamiliar riding the roads around here on another red ATV?" I was hoping he would say yes, and he could point us in the right direction.

"Can't remember what day it was, but there was a young fellow on an ATV riding along the side of the road. I paid little attention to him because I was looking for my own ATV. When I slowed down, he took off for the woods down the street."

"How far down the street was this?" I question as my pulse accelerates.

"About a quarter-mile, same side of the road we are on now. A lot of kids ride ATVs in these woods. Is there something wrong?"

"No, John. Take your ATV home."

"I will try when I get it started." John rubs his neck as if frustrated.

I walk over to the ATV, "Let me help." Three seconds is all it takes. The ATV purrs like a kitten. When I turn around, everyone is standing with their mouths hanging open and their eyes wide. "What? My dad taught me how to change tires and hotwire cars." I shrug my shoulders and start walking back to the car.

Taylor and Ivey chuckle behind me when we meet up with Johnson and Rufus. "How'd it go, Sheriff? I heard you talking with someone."

"We found John Smith as he was trying to hotwire his own ATV. It seems John reported the ATV missing to the sheriff's office last week. He came looking for it and found it. Mr. Smith was nice enough to point us in another direction about a quarter-mile down the road. It seems John spotted someone on an ATV. I thought it might be his. He slowed down to get a better look, and the guy took off."

"Let's go back to the name, John Smith. You really believe his name is John Smith?" Deputy Johnson questions with a slight grin.

"Yes, I do. Taylor can verify it because he saw the guy's ID. It's official." I answer, shaking my head, thinking about how hard it would be to grow up with a name like John Smith. "Load up, guys. We are moving down the road."

Tuttle calls while we are moving locations. "Sheriff, did the box truck owner call back?"

"No. Neither Darlene nor the truck owner returned my calls. Can you try the truck owner again? Also, find out who owns the warehouse. I'd like to speak to them too."

As I am pulling off the road, my car slips toward the ditch. The dirt in these parts of the county is loose on the shoulders of the roads. If you're not careful, your vehicle will slide into a rainwater runoff ditch. I exited on the street side, which prevented me from tumbling into the ditch. I wave Johnson and Taylor down the road to more secure parking.

"We will search the same as we did last time. Taylor and I in the lead. The rest of you will follow."

With the sun still shining, we start again on yet another search. The grass is still blowing in the breeze, which helps. Rufus has his nose down, and he is off. He seems to enjoy his time in the outdoors. His tail wags constantly, and his eyes are bright. We fan out a little to cover more ground.

The woods on this side of the road are rockier, and less light seeps between the branches. Travel is slow because of the terrain, and I look at my phone. One bar for cell service, and that always sends shivers up my spine.

"What's wrong, Sheriff? Your facial expression is strange." Ivey asks with concern in her voice.

"I always stay abreast of communication just in case it's needed. There is only one bar of service on my phone. That doesn't give me a lot of confidence if we need help."

Taylor pipes up, "We'll be fine. There are four of us against one. Surely, one of us can get a clean shot."

"Something is making me uneasy, and I never ignore my gut. It's saved me on more than one occasion." I offer.

"Yeah, Sheriff. I remember. What do you want to do? Want to stop and turn back?"

Two steps later, Rufus lets out a bark. He alerts onto something. We tread over to his location. Johnson has a strange look on his face as he points to Rufus's find. Following the line, I notice an object lying beside a small stream of water.

"Is that what I think it is? Tell me I'm wrong." I put my gloves on and reach down and pull a boot from the water, and it looks like Tonya's black tasseled boot. My heart sinks as I consider why the killer is taking the victims' shoes. The lack of shoes is an old-fashioned way of preventing hostages from running away. It is hard to run without footwear, especially in the woods. The rocks and sticks on the ground will tear a person's feet to shreds. "Walk around this area and look for additional signs of Tonya. If she is in the woods, we need to find her now."

We scour the area on both sides of the small stream and discover Tonya's other boot on the backside of a rock grouping. "Sheriff, this boot might have blood on it. See the drop here. It is brownish-red. I'll bag this boot separately so they can check it."

"Good call, Taylor. Here's another evidence bag for you."

Ivey reaches out and takes it from me. She holds it open for Taylor to drop the boot inside. Ivey hands Taylor a black marker so he can sign the chain of custody. We can't take the chance of messing this case up because someone was sloppy with evidence collection.

"We found Tonya's boots, so do we think Tonya was in the woods, or did someone place the boots in the woods?" I asked because I wanted to know the other's thoughts.

Ivey glances around before responding, "I can't imagine anyone walking this far into the woods to place a pair of boots next to a stream hoping to throw us off a trail. No one comes back here, so it's not likely they are trying to confuse the search. I think Tonya was here."

"I agree. Tonya wore these boots into the woods and left with none unless she is still in the woods somewhere. We found no homes or camping sites anywhere. So, where is she hiding? What's on the other side of the woods?" Taylor wonders.

"Taylor, Tonya's hiding place is unknown, as is what's on the other side of these woods. I will check with county records to see who owns the property. Can you do your thing with the satellite imagery and see what you can find about these woods?"

"Absolutely, Sheriff. I'll start on that as soon as we can get back to civilization."

We walk to our vehicles in silence. Tonya's boots were a blow to my heart. I wanted to find Tonya and return her to her parents. Now, I'm not so sure I can do that. Something tells me she is dead, but until I have a body, I push forward. Giving up is not an option.

As we reach the edge of the woods, the hair on my neck prickles again. I feel as if someone is watching us, so I inspect the area without being obvious. Could the killer be in the area and follow us? Deputy Taylor recognizes my resistance to escape the woods. He peers through the woods too and sees nothing. He nods in affirmation as we walk out into the sunshine.

"Thanks, Rufus." I lean in the vehicle to give him a rubdown and a kiss on the nose before Johnson pulls away from the search site.

"Where are you two headed?" I ask Taylor and Ivey. It is midafternoon, but I don't want to go back to the office. My body is calling for a hot shower and a cup of coffee. There are too many thoughts swirling in my head. Quiet time is what I need to help me sort out my ideas, and I can get more of that at home than the office allows.

"I'm going to the office and check on the satellite imagery. I'll call you when I finish. Ivey can ride with me. Want to meet for dinner?"

"Check in with me later. I'll let you know. I'm not sure if I'm going home or to the office yet because I'm not feeling too festive at the moment." Closing the car door, I realize how alone I am. At times, it's nice, but other times, like now, it's not. Right now, I want to scream. Why did this killer bring these murders to my county? I need an answer to that question. No, I deserve an answer to that question.

Taylor and Ivey pull out onto the road before me. They are talking and smiling at each other. At least there are some good things to come out of dangerous situations. Once this case is over, I hope they keep their relationship going.

As I sit on the roadside, I call Maggie and advise her to post a BOLO for Tonya. Once Maggie hears the update about the boots, she sniffs. "Maggie, I'm upset too, but we have to keep searching. At present, Tonya's whereabouts are still unknown. We need the public's help to bring her home. Any return call from Tonya's parents or Darlene?"

"Not yet," Maggie answers.

The call ends on a sour note. Maggie is crying, I want to cry, and I still have nothing to show. We've spent hours searching the woods, and all we have gathered is footwear. Who is this killer? Are they from these parts of the state? If not, how did they become familiar with these roads?

I drive to the office, going over the case in my head. Finding abandoned shoes and boots are troubling as this generally means the victims are dead. So, why did the killer place the shoes in the woods? It's a wonder we found them at all—it was pure luck. It involved no investigative skills. A passerby described the location, and we took it from there.

No one speaks in the office, and everyone keeps their eyes down. When I close the door to my office, my desk phone rings, and I waver on whether to answer. In the end, I comply, but I hit the speaker button, so I don't have to hold the handset.

"Hi, Darlene. Thanks for calling back. No, we haven't found Tonya yet. Would you mind answering a few questions about cheerleading? Tonya was a competition cheerleader, right? Do you know if she was a member of a closed group on a social media platform?"

"Yes, she was a competition cheerleader and a member of several social media groups. A lot of the cheerleaders join groups. The cheerleaders compare routines, travel plans, and just ordinary stuff. Why are you asking, Sheriff?"

"We are looking into leads, and this popped up. The other murdered girls were also cheerleaders and being on competition squads allowed the girls to travel to multiple states depending on competition location. Are you a member of the closed group that Tonya belonged to?"

"No. I'm sure Tonya would have let me join, but I didn't see the point since I wasn't part of the cheerleading group."

"I'm not savvy on the social media stuff. How can I gain access to her account? We want to see some posts and compare them with the other girls' accounts."

"Her mom might know her login and password because she used to monitor Tonya's time on the phone during school. Other than that, I can't help you." Darlene states.

"Thanks for calling back. If you think of anything else, call me."

Leaning back in my chair, it stuns me. Every phone call and every conversation is a roadblock. Bud will receive the warrants for Tonya's social media accounts soon. Those accounts are crucial. Tonya's parents are ignoring me, and I don't know why. Some questions require answers. One more phone call. If no response, I will show up on their doorstep.

With the phone propped up between my head and shoulder, I listen to it ring. My patience is running low. I slam the phone down, grab my gun and bag, and head toward the door. As I reach for the knob, it turns. Stepping back so I won't get slapped in the face by the door, I'm surprised to see Bud standing there with papers in his hand. "Going somewhere, Sheriff?" Bud asks with a grin.

"Yes. I am going to Tonya's house. Her parents are ignoring me. No one has interviewed them yet, and time is up. What brings you by?"

"I brought you a present." Bud grins.

"Really? A present for me? You're giving me a piece of paper?"

"Read it, Sheriff. It's your warrant for Tonya's social media accounts. Are you ready to search the internet?"

"You bet I am. I could hug you right now. Thanks for bringing the warrants over. When can we get started if you are still willing to help me?"

Bud checks his watch, "right after you have supper with me."

Chapter 8

"I'll take you up on that. Let Ivey know what we are doing. If she and Taylor want to join us, they can, but you are mine after supper. I've been waiting on the warrants."

Bud grins and heads over to the bullpen to find Ivey. Just as I am closing my door, my phone rings. I contemplate not answering, but duty wins that battle again. Tonya's dad is the caller, and he apologizes for not calling sooner. They have been staying with family and just returned home today. My number was on their caller ID. Expressing my concern with Tonya's disappearance is more challenging than I thought. By the sound of their voice, they lost hope for Tonya's return. He advises they will be available tomorrow to answer questions. We set a time for me to come by their house around ten in the morning.

Ivey is leaning against the door frame when I place the phone in the cradle. "Was that Tonya's parents?"

"Finally. That was her dad. They were staying with family members trying to get away from the media, I suppose. He's agreed to meet me tomorrow at ten. Want to join me?"

"I'd love to go. I'm not convinced they will shed any light on the investigation, but we need to confirm that. Bud told us he has your warrants, and you are starting tonight. I hope that leads somewhere. Bud is setting up another one of our team members to work on the other girls' accounts, and once those are running, we can compare the accounts for similarities. This might be our best lead yet, and we need to thank you for that." Ivey conveys her appreciation.

"We need answers. I don't care how we get them. We must stop this killer. He has killed too many young girls already. Who knows how many it will be before someone captures him? I don't want him thinking he can keep playing in my county." My reply comes across harsher than I intend, but Ivey gets my point. "Bud and I are going to dinner. Are you coming? I want to get back so we can start on the social media search."

Ivey shakes her head from side to side as she explains, "Dinner will be a little later for us. Taylor is completing reports, and I am checking in with the FBI office for an update. We will catch up later tonight."

Bud leans on the trunk of my car as I exit the sheriff's office. "How long have you been out here?"

"Not too long. Why?" Bud asks with concern in his voice.

"Just spent ten minutes searching for you. Ivey is giving an update to the FBI office, and I didn't know if you wanted to take part." I sound irritated, and I am.

"She can handle it. I'm her back-up, and

we need to get these social media account searches started. So, off to dinner, alone." I see a twinkle in Bud's eye. What do I make of that?

The night turns out good. Bud shares stories from his childhood, and I do the same. I share memories from years past. Now I know why I don't think about the past. It conjures up memories of my dad. I try not to dwell on it, but some days, it hits me hard. With Tonya still missing, the murders, the killer still on the run, it is hitting harder today than most days.

After supper, we drove back to the office. As we walked closer to the sheriff's office side door, we heard noises coming from inside. I glance at Bud, and he walks up to the back door and motions me to get behind him. "Really, Bud? We are standing at the door to my sheriff's office. I got this." Just as I turn the knob, something heavy strikes the door. I jump back, and Bud breaks my fall.

"My turn," Bud says in my ear. He reaches for the door, turns the knob, waits three seconds, and opens the door. As he steps over the threshold, a giant tennis ball strikes him mid-chest. Then Rufus is coming at us full force.

"Rufus, slow down!" I yell. He acts like he doesn't hear me and unleashes kisses on both of us as we lie sprawled on the floor laughing.

"I am so sorry. I didn't know you were coming back after dinner. Rufus needed to release some of his energy. Rufus, please apologize." Deputy Johnson instructs the dog. The dog doesn't quit until he places sloppy kisses on each of us. "Apology accepted. Just be careful that a citizen doesn't come through the door and get clobbered. We would be privy to a mess." I advise halfheartedly since few people use the side door.

Bud and I make it safely into my office and shut the door. With an extra table added to my office, there will be plenty of room for us. Once we set up everything, Bud leads me into the social media world. He spends an hour briefing me on what to look for and what to ignore. We start with Tonya's information. I have one account open on my computer, and Bud has another. There have been no postings made since the day she disappeared. Tonya is very social as she stays involved with several groups. I wonder how she accomplishes anything with the number of posts she makes each day. She must be a fantastic multi-tasker.

"Do you see anything that stands out on her personal page? I don't so far." I ask.

"No, I don't. Her personal page is friends and family. We need to look deeper, something dealing with cheerleading competitions. The posts will be short, not like her personal page."

My body needs to move, and my brain needs a break. We have been sitting at the computer for hours, and I am not a sitter. Now, I question my idea. Was social media the best way to find the killer? The coach didn't send over the competition schedule. That might be our best bet.

"Bud, the school cheerleading coach, didn't send over the competition schedule. Now I doubt the social media angle. This is time-consuming. Let me try to get her on the phone again."

Coach Turner answers on the second ring. "Hi, Sheriff. I didn't forget the schedule. I couldn't find mine, but a peer sent one over. It should be in your inbox now."

"Thanks, Coach Turner, for your help." I end the call because I want to see the schedule. Thirty seconds later, my email alerts me to a new message. I open it and glance at the locations for the competitions. Coach Turner told the truth as the tournaments occurred across the southeast. The next scheduled event is ten days from now in Tallahassee.

With my finger pointing to a future date, I say, "Look at this. The schedule says the next cheerleading event is in Tallahassee. That seems odd since the girls found in the ditch were from Tallahassee."

"My suggestion is to let the FBI attend the tournaments and monitor the people involved with the cheerleaders. The killer contacts these girls somehow. Otherwise, Tonya would never leave school. I mean, the killer didn't walk into the school and kidnap her. She left school on her own volition." Bud remarks.

"Can you make it happen with the FBI in Tallahassee? I am optimistic that it will give us a fresh lead. What are the locations of the other murders? We can compare those deaths with this schedule and see if we have a match."

"I can handle both requests. The FBI will put a team together in Tallahassee, and Ivey and I will head it up. Will you go with us?" Bud questions with his eyes pleading me to say yes.

"Depends on what is happening around here. If we have not located Tonya, I won't leave, but I will be here when you come back." I watch Bud's face relax. He tensed while waiting for my answer. My insides quiver, and that's something that hasn't happened in a long time.

"I'll work on the Florida trip first thing in the morning. I've pulled the records on the other murders. Are you too tired to read a couple? We can write down names and locations and go from there."

We spend the better part of two hours writing, erasing, and writing more. Just when we think our system is working, it falls apart. Without giving up, we finally get a few of the victims on paper. So far, nothing matches the place of residence, school, or location of the body.

"Bud, I'm exhausted. I need to head home. Can I drop you at the hotel? We can start again in the morning." I mutter.

"It has been a long day. I wouldn't mind a nap myself. We'll leave the papers and be ready to jump back in tomorrow."

After dropping Bud off at the hotel, my mind races with so many thoughts. I don't want to wait ten days before the events take place in Tallahassee. I don't want to spend endless hours scouring social media accounts, and I don't want someone to murder Tonya. I do not wish to speak with the press. My car must have driven itself home because I can't say I remember getting back. That's when I realize this case consumes me. It's scary when you arrive home, but you're not sure how you managed it.

I realize I haven't checked my mailbox in days. It's pitch black outside, but I walk to the curb anyway. All sorts of nighttime creatures are roaming around when something moves in my peripheral vision. My hands fly to my side and rest over my gun. What is that? Is that a person? Too tired to follow, I grab the mail and jog into the house, but I glance over my shoulder just to make sure no one is following me.

I fall into bed, thinking sleep will come quickly. However, once I lie down, my brain won't stop. The case keeps me awake for longer than I want. Once my eyelids close, sleep comes, but I toss and turn. With only a few hours of troubled sleep, I don't recognize the sound of my ringing phone. The ringing stops and starts again before I grab it. I listen to the caller and sit straight up in the bed.

"Slow down, Ivey. Repeat that." My

heart races as I listen to Ivey describe the next crime scene.

"Bud and I are driving to Mobile, Alabama. A fisherman found four bodies under a pier in Mobile Bay. Same MO as the other finds. We will call you when we get there. Take care, Sheriff."

Even though it's still in the wee hours of the morning, sleep will not come back. I make coffee and sit in my recliner, rehashing my conversation with Ivey. Bud and Ivey are driving to Mobile, Alabama, toward more bodies. The killer is prolific if nothing else. Now that there is a possibility of losing Ivey and Bud, I don't like the idea. It's funny how life works sometimes and who comes into your life when you're not expecting it.

Entering the sheriff's office in the early morning hours is surreal. It is breathtakingly quiet. I survey the bullpen area then I cruise through our dispatcher's site. All is running smoothly, so I go into my office and shut the door. Tonya's parents are not expecting me until ten.

I grab another coffee and work on the papers that Bud and I left on the table just a few hours before. This process is tedious. Time spent rewriting the graph is well worth it, and I tape the charts to the office wall. I write the victim's name with address, crime scene location, school, and if they are members of a cheerleading squad. I print the notes in black ink, with each descriptive word written in a different color. Once that is complete, I use a red marker to draw lines to matching traits. I'm still not done two hours later, but I don't want to reschedule my visit with Tonya's parents. The graphs will be here after the interview. I close my door and head to the car.

My cell phone rings as soon as the car starts. The caller ID shows its Ivey. "Hi, Ivey. How's it going?"

"It is gruesome. I hate water deaths. There are four girls, same MO as your victims, bound, gagged, and shoeless. The coroner will have a tough time verifying the time of death. The sea creatures did a number on the bodies. Bud and I will stay here for two days at the most. If the killer's dumpsites remain the same, these girls are not from here. Once the coroner conducts the autopsies, we will complete our reports and drive back to you."

"Thanks for the update. I am on my way to see Tonya's parents. They didn't seem happy to speak with me, which I find odd. Most parents want to see law enforcement immediately after a child goes missing. I'll let you know how it goes." Our call ends, and I ponder the latest.

Four more victims are unnerving. If these girls are members of a cheerleading squad, I will bet my job on the killer being associated with the competitions somehow. That is the only aspect of these girls' lives that correlate with one another. The problem is how to find the killer. There are a lot of competitions occurring at the same time across the southeast. That line of thinking will have to wait.

The Zons live in a residential neighborhood in the county. Although the houses are cookie-cutter, the builder used four original plans throughout the community. The builder flipped some homes, so the garages are on opposite sides of the houses, presumably to add character. The Zon house is noticeable with the driveway full of cars. I park in the street next to the curb, and I am careful not to block the mailbox.

With the front door ajar, I hear talking. There are several people in the house. I was only expecting the Zons. Apparently, someone watched me walk up onto the porch because two young smiling faces meet me at the door. "Hi, I'm Sheriff Steele. Are Mr. and Mrs. Zon home?"

"Yes, come in." The door opens into a family room of sorts. The room is full of people. I try to decide who the Zons are, but I can't, so I wait for the introductions.

"Sheriff, I'm Tonya's dad, Terry Zon. Please follow me to the kitchen."

Once I'm seated at the kitchen table, Tonya's mom enters. She is a petite lady with long black hair and red puffy eyes. She does not speak to me, and I let it pass for now.

"Thank you for taking the time to meet. I

need to ask a few questions. Was Tonya dating anyone seriously? If so, how was their relationship?" I ask the questions staring at Mr. Zon.

Mr. Zon answers without looking at his wife. He is the one in control of his family. Mrs. Zon doesn't lift her eyes. "She didn't have a boyfriend. Tonya dated now and then but nothing serious."

"Was Tonya involved in a competition cheerleading squad?"

"Yes." Tonya's dad is a man of few words.

"Ok. Did she ever mention to either of you if she met someone while at a tournament?"

Finally, the mom opens her mouth. "The last event Tonya took part in was in Alabama, but that was months ago. She was concentrating on bringing her math grade up before exams. Tonya's next scheduled tournament was in Tallahassee. Did something happen at the competition?"

"We can't confirm that just yet. My questions are part of the ongoing investigation." Trying to keep the conversation flowing, I move on to another question, "Is there a chance Tonya was a part of a social media group for cheerleaders?"

Both Tonya's mom and dad shrug their shoulders. They did not understand what their child did on the internet. The dad paid for the cell phone, and that's it. He definitely didn't monitor the usage like he did when she received her first phone. . The lack of supervision by a parent is something that baffles me. How can a parent expect kids to make wise decisions if they don't know what they do and who they do it with?

"One last question—did Tonya mention a recent friend to you or a family member?"

Tonya's parents' glance at each other, then her dad leaves the table and walks into the family room. Mr. Zon returns with a young girl in tow. "This is Rosemary, Tonya's cousin. She might help answer that question."

"Hi, Rosemary. I'm Sheriff Steele. Did Tonya tell you about a new friend?"
Rosemary looks up at Mr. Zon before continuing, "Tonya told me she talked with a new guy a few weeks back. I don't know if it was during her trip to Alabama or not. Also, Tonya said the guy told her she would make a great hair model. That's all I know."

"That is important information, Rosemary. Thank you for sharing." After I jot notes in my book, I ask, "Is there anything else you can think of that might help? The smallest thing has led to arrests before, so don't think something might be inconsequential. I need to hear everything." I pause, letting my statement sink in, but no one speaks.

When no one offered anything, I asked to see Tonya's room. It helps to learn about the missing individual. Rosemary looks to Mr. Zon for an answer. He nods, so Rosemary escorts me to Tonya's room. As I enter, I survey the room from the doorway. There is a twin bed tucked into the corner of the room against the left wall. The room offers a compact closet and one single window.

Tonya used a window seat in the bay window for storage. All of her school books were there, along with a backpack. I walked over to it and peeked inside, but it was empty. As I continued the room inspection, I noticed there were no pictures of family or friends.

"Rosemary, does Tonya have pictures of friends in here?" As I glance around, I see none.

"None that I know about because she keeps most of them on her phone."

After I saw Tonya's room, Mr. Zon walks me out to my car. "Please call if you think of anything. We will get a warrant for Tonya's cell phone records. I'll call with any updates."

He doesn't answer, only nods. I start my car and pull away from the curb. There are nosey neighbors, and some are blatant as they stand at their windows, and at others, curtains move as I pass. The meeting was fruitful since I gleaned two items of interest. Tonya was a member of a competitive cheer squad, and she met a new friend. Too bad Bud wasn't with me. He could get that warrant faster than me.

Back at the sheriff's office, I add the

recent information to the murder board. Looking at it, it impresses me as it is almost full. If we don't arrest this killer soon, the sheriff's office will need to dip into the budget to buy a new board. Now, with new leads, the graphs need additional work, and I need a warrant for Tonya's cell phone. My hope is Tonya spent time on the phone with this new guy. If so, with his number, we can ping his cell phone. Then, we can bring him in for questioning.

Chapter 9

My notebook flips open when I slide it over, and I glimpse a scribble. The word 'model' pops out at me. I take a highlighter and mark over the term. Did that have anything to do with the case? Is that the lure the killer uses to meet these girls? I add the word to the board. Somehow, we need to ask the other victims' parents and friends if any of the victims mentioned a new friend and the term "model."

Excitement courses through my veins. I have things to share with Ivey and Bud, but they are away. It hasn't even been twenty-four hours since they left for Mobile, and I already feel alone. Without knowing their schedules, I don't dare call to share my news. They are working on a new scene, and it sounds worse than mine. I've only worked a few water deaths in my time in law enforcement, and they weren't pleasant. Water can do some strange things to a human body. I didn't envy Bud and Ivey in the least.

Bud and Ivey aren't here, but Taylor and Tuttle are working today. "Maggie, call Taylor and Tuttle. I need to see them at their convenience. No rush."

While waiting for the guys, I backtrack to the graphs and count the number of victims. We are at the halfway mark. "Sheriff, what you got for us?"

Taylor and Tuttle come running. I carry a tender spot for both men. When I look up to see them standing side by side, I snicker because they are wider than the door. "Come in and shut the door. I have news to share."

Everyone settles in, and I walk over to the murder board. "You've added more items, Sheriff." Taylor notices the change right away. That is not surprising since he has a keen eye.

"You're right. I met with Tonya Zon's parents earlier. Tonya was a competitive cheer squad member, and Tonya's cousin confirmed she had a new guy friend. Supposedly, this new guy friend mentioned to Tonya about being a model."

"That is interesting, Sheriff. Any idea who this guy might be or where they met?" Tuttle asks as he enters notes in his book.

"No, we don't know his identity yet. I think a warrant for Tonya's cell phone will be the next step. She was in Alabama for her last competition a month ago. Her next scheduled meet was in Tallahassee. So, what am I missing?"

"I see nothing missing. Without a description or name of this guy, the only way to track him is by using Tonya's cell. What did her parents say about her social media presence?" Taylor questions the social media aspect.

"Tonya's parents had no clue about her social media accounts." Every time I say that it makes me mad. Why can't parents take the time to know their children's friends? I pause before I throw out another idea that has been bothering me.

In a curious tone, Taylor asks, "What's troubling you, Sheriff? I can see you are working on something."

"Yes, I am Taylor. Could the idea of becoming a model be the promise the girls are after when they meet up with this stranger?"

Tuttle jumps in, "That is a great angle to search the social media accounts of all the victims. Are there modeling crews at these cheer competitions?"

The ringing phone jars everyone out of their brainstorming time. I grab the phone, take a big breath, sit back, and listen while Bud gives an update on the Alabama scene. It turns out, Alabama is the same as the rest. There are four bodies, tied, bound, gagged, and shoeless. Someone found the girls under a pier at Mobile Bay. One bit of news is a camera on the pier captured a box truck turning into the parking lot. Bud and Ivey are waiting for the video. The medical examiner confirms he will have the autopsies completed by tomorrow, and Bud and Ivey will be back the day after tomorrow to continue the case. Bud says goodbye and that he will call me later. As I lay the phone in the cradle, I am giddy at the thought of Bud calling me tonight at home.

After the call, I update Taylor and Tuttle on the Alabama scene. Tuttle asks the obvious question, "How many murders have the same attributes?"

"I'll ask Bud or Ivey for the total. There are seven for sure. Our three found on Shallow Bottoms Road, and the four girls found in Alabama. This killer is relentless. It makes me wonder if two killers are working in tandem. I'll let you know when I get the video of the box truck too."

Now, Taylor has a puzzled expression when he states, "So, let me get this right, you think modeling is the lure for the girls, and now you added a second killer. Does that sum it up?"

"Are you saying it sounds crazy? Or do you think it is workable?" I question.

"Absolutely, it is. It sounds more plausible than anything else I've heard or thought. What about you, Tuttle?" Taylor turns his head to face Tuttle.

As we wait for Tuttle's reply, dispatch interrupts our meeting with a call requesting Taylor and Tuttle for crowd control at a forest fire. "Dispatch, this is Sheriff Steele. Please repeat the call."

"Sheriff, a caller reports a forest fire burning down the road from the Snappy Mart. The call came from the parking lot of the mart. The caller advises the fire is raging."

"Taylor, Tuttle, go now. Call once you get to the scene. Let me know if we need others." I bark instructions to the guy's backs as they race out of the office.

113

As I watch the deputies run, my gut clenches. Is it a coincidence the woods are on fire in the same area we searched for Tonya? Somehow, I know it's not. I try to concentrate on other chores, but my mind keeps wandering back to Tonya. If the Corp of Engineers owns the property, shouldn't the Department of Natural Resources be fighting the fire too? "Dispatch, Sheriff Steele. Has someone notified DNR of the fire?"

"Sheriff, yes. With the breeze, the fire has doubled in size in less than an hour. With the dry brush, DNR called in a full brush assignment. The fire department is putting water on it, but it's not doing much to slow the fire's progression. One fire truck had to return to the station to refill its water tank. The others will follow at some point. DNR will cut a firebreak around the outside of the fire to help contain it. If the fire jumps the road, we are in trouble. I will update as reports come."

Speechless, I lay the mic down on my desk and put my head in my hands. Why do I feel so helpless? I've never thought I couldn't do the job until this case came along and threw me out of kilter. If the fire crosses the road, it will take out the Snappy Mart and a few cabins.

"Deputies Taylor and Tuttle, how do you read me?" I repeat several times before I give up and reach for my cell phone. The call goes to Taylor's voicemail. Tuttle answers on the fourth ring.

"Sheriff, this situation is grave. We evacuated the cabin residents below the Snappy Mart. There are cars parked along the road to watch the fire. We closed the road on both sides of the fire from additional onlookers. However, the bulldozer needed for the fire break hasn't made it to the scene. I'm on one end of the road, and Taylor is on the other."

"I'm on the way." Placing my mic in its holder, I gun the engine and make my way to the fire.

The fire lights the sky up like a torch. Fire is an amazing spectacle to watch. Flames twist in the breeze as they reach for the clouds. Glowing embers dance around the sky in all directions as they make their way back to the ground. No wonder people pulled off the road to watch. The fire is an incredible sight, even though I dread the ending. I made it to the scene just as the dozer pulled in. Maybe now, they can get a handle on the fire and stop it before embers jump the road and start another fire. At least, where the fire began is desolate. Or, last, I remember, it was. No one has ever lived on that side of the road where the fire burns, that I recall. People hunt that property in the fall and winter. Deer and other creatures run wild in those parts.

"Tuttle, how are you holding up? Want me to take a turn standing out here?" I ask.

"No, Sheriff, I'm okay. Now that the dozer is here, I expect the fire to be out shortly.

The cabins should be safe now unless the wind changes direction again."

"Residents can't go back until the fire is completely out. Okay?"

"10-4," replies Tuttle.

I walk toward the Snappy Mart parking lot. It's awkward to see so many people gazing at the fire and talking amongst themselves. One person asks another, "Do you think the fire was deliberate?"

The other answers, "Surely not. Who would want to burn down those woods? Everyone knows there is nothing out there."

As I walk past the twosome, I overhear their conversation, and I lift a small prayer begging God not to let anyone perish in the fire. Answers to the fire would be forthcoming soon enough. The investigation would seek to find out: where did it start, why did it start, and who started it?

Taylor leans against his car, beads of sweat rolling down the side of his face. "Why are you sweating?" I question.

"When we first arrived, I ran toward the fire to see if anyone was in trouble. I swear a heard a girl cry for help, but the fire was so intense I couldn't get close enough."

"Oh, Taylor. Could it be you thought you heard things in the rush? I hope not, but I will tell you I have a bad feeling about this fire. I'm not sure if it is a diversion or a crime scene. We'll be here when the fire is out, and we'll get a look." I lean back on the car beside Taylor and cringe with the thought of what we might find.

Taylor and I watch the fire department put out hot spots along the roadside. A few of the onlooker's rush to move their vehicles for fear of the cars catching fire. The only area scorched was the woods. The watchers pile in cars and leave once the firefighters douse the fire. As everyone leaves, we gather around my car and make plans to walk into the burned area. Taylor shares with Tuttle his experience on their arrival, and it shocks Tuttle because he heard nothing like Taylor described.

Department of Natural Resources personnel scour the area as we enter the fire zone. They scatter a few groups around the burned area, searching for the origin. They snap pictures and turn over debris before moving on to a new spot. DNR officers snap a photo at each location, turn over the earth, and take the time to jot down notes several times. Deputy Taylor questions me about the notes. "Wonder what their notes are about? Everything appears the same. It's all scorched."

I share, "The fire department and DNR officers are trying to locate the point of origin. When they find it, they will know what started the fire. If the fire is arson, that's a crime, of course, so we would press charges against the perpetrator once we capture them."

Tuttle continues the conversation, "If the perpetrator turns out to be our killer, they can just add arson to the murder charges."

We are walking deeper into the burned area when my cell phone rings. "Sheriff Steele." When I answer, my stomach turns a flip as I listen to the caller. "We are approximately 100 yards away from the stream. Let them know we are on our way."

"Follow me, deputies. There is a body in the stream." Once the statement is out of my mouth, I remember Deputy Taylor's experience. "Taylor, we don't know who it is yet. Even if it is Tonya, there would have been nothing you could have done to save her. No one would have been able to enter the burning woods without putting themselves in jeopardy."

Tuttle and I glance at Taylor while we walk. His expression is pure grief. His eyes turn dark as he clenches his jaws. He is always the rock of our group. I place my hand on his arm, "Taylor, you did the right thing. Never question yourself on that. Okay?"

"Sheriff, I don't know. I just don't know what to think right now." Taylor replies with downcast eyes.

There is a crowd of people standing around the stream upon our arrival. They appear to be comparing notes. "Here you go, Sheriff. She is over there on the other side of the rock." I can't conjure up the words to respond to the DNR guy, so I nod while walking over to the body and try to hold myself upright. Her feet are visible first, then her clothes, and finally, her face. The body is Tonya Zon's. Someone shot her in the head, just like the other victims.

"Guys, take photos before the medical examiner arrives. Tonya's parents need to know as soon as possible. It's obvious we are looking at the same killer. However, the fire confuses me."

Tuttle and Taylor take photos while I call Doc James. He will arrive within thirty minutes. So, we have thirty minutes to inspect the scene. I walk over to the group of people and ask the obvious, "Did you locate the origin and what started the fire?"

The lead DNR officer replies, "An accelerant, possibly gasoline, started the fire. The origin is 50 yards northwest of here. I can tell you, if the victim had not been in the stream, the fire would have completely burned her body. Lucky for her family, she was. At least they get closure now."

"I suppose you could look at it that way," I reply. There is nothing worse than telling parents their child is dead, especially at the hands of a murderer. Taylor calls me over to the body.

"Here you go, Sheriff," as he points to the back of Tonya's head. "Is that an exit would?"

I take a closer look. "It might be. It looks like dried blood in her hair. As soon as Doc James turns the body, we will know for sure. My hope is Tonya died of a gunshot and not from smoke inhalation from the fire. At least the gunshot would be a quick death."

My throat is scratchy and hurting because of the smoke I've swallowed. As I walk the crime scene's perimeter, I hear someone yelling from farther into the woods. "Tuttle stay with the body. Taylor, you're with me."

Both of us are breathing heavily farther into the woods we travel. Once we reach the screamer, we notice his find. Another set of ATV tracks head away from the fire. "Great find. Any idea where these tracks might lead? I thought this area was nothing but woods."

"It is. That's why this is odd. There are a hundred or more acres back here, and it's all woods. A logging company cut the timber twenty years ago, and nothing has happened here since," a DNR guy states.

Taylor walks a little farther down the tracks, searching for anything of interest. I watch as he turns over the brush and moves tree branches. "Sheriff, are you carrying an evidence bag? I found a candy bar wrapper."

"Nice work, Taylor. Here you go."

I answer my cell phone and listen as Tuttle advises Doc James and his crew have arrived. They are preparing to turn Tonya's body. "Ask him to wait for us. We are walking back to you now."

Listening to my conversation, Taylor stands as he is ready to walk over to Tonya. "I still think a girl called for help. However, if someone shot Tonya, I don't see how it was her unless she was running from the killer when she screamed. Tonya might still be with us if I had reached her in time."

"Taylor, I told you not to think like that. There was nothing you could have done to save her. You would have put yourself in danger, and that wouldn't have solved any problems. You made the right decision."

The rest of the trip is silent. Neither one of us know what to say since the dreaded discussion with Tonya's parents' looms over our heads. Once I see the body, I will go straight over to their house and tell them the news. After we notify her parents, we will call Mr. Hales, so he can make plans to have a grief counselor at the school. The sooner this happens, the better for all involved.

Doc James turns Tonya's body over, and the confirmation is quick. She has a bullet hole in her forehead, and now we have our fourth victim. I glance at Taylor, and I see his jaws clench as he grits his teeth. This killer has him seething mad. "Taylor, I'm going to Tonya's parents to deliver the news. You can stay with Doc James and Tuttle to finish up the scene."

"Sheriff, I'd prefer to go with you. I know the family, too, and it's my duty to deliver the news."

"If that's what you want, I'd like the company. Tuttle, you're in charge of the scene. If you need me, call my cell. Keep this off the radio." Tuttle nods in agreement, and we say our goodbyes to Doc James.

The rest of the afternoon is a blur of activity. After speaking with the Zons about Tonya and notifying Mr. Hale, Taylor asks me to drop him off at the sheriff's office, and I continue home. I can't talk to another person. Well, maybe one other person, but Bud has his own troubles.

Chapter 10

I pour myself a ginger ale at home as I don't partake in alcohol, and I sit in my recliner. My job requires me too always be ready. The TV remains silent for fear of what I might see. After a few minutes of solitude, the smell of smoke on my clothes totally engulfs me. A fire smell is not pleasant when it brings back memories of death. A shower helps with the smell but not with the memories. The quicker I clean up, the better I will feel, or so I hope. Two scrub downs and one hair washing later, my body smells better, but my emotions worsen. I face a dilemma of death and hunger. The only items of food in my kitchen are peanut butter and eggs. Supper turns into scrambled eggs again.

This day just wouldn't end, so I collapse into bed early. While reading a book, my phone rings, but where is it? Dashing through the house, I remember taking it with me for my shower. My phone is in my pants pocket. I answer it on the last ring, and I am pleasantly surprised at the caller.

Bud calls to check on me and the case. I give a rundown of the events from the day. He expresses sympathy for finding Tonya, and then he questions my mental state. I am honest about my feelings about the case, especially Tonya. Bud shares that he is looking forward to seeing me tomorrow. Of course, I agree. Bud suggests dinner together outside of the county. He wants to talk about a few things, but he won't let me ask questions. So, I doze off to sleep, dreaming of Bud and what he wants to discuss.

The next morning comes too quickly. I'm not ready to face the day, but duty calls. I roll into the sheriff's department and enter through the back door. The office is relatively calm, which helps because I have to complete Tonya's death report. That's the most challenging part of doing a report. You must relive the scene, no matter how hard you try to put it out of your mind.

After finishing the report, I glance at the whiteboard and remember I need to add information. By adding Tonya's name to the victim list, the total stands at four. So, we have identified our four victims. Agent Ivey calls mid-morning and discusses Tonya. She also states additional agents are researching the previous victims regarding any connection with competition cheer squads. The FBI teams will travel to Tallahassee for the next cheerleading competition tournament in three days. Then Ivey adds they will travel to Tallahassee before returning to her because the FBI wants their eyes on the set-up. The team will go later. Ivey hears the disappointment in my voice, and she assures me it will be no longer than two days, and they will be back.

Another two days to figure out what Bud

wants to discuss. I hope our feelings are mutual. With our jobs, I'm not sure how we will make this work. But, when you want something bad enough, you make it work.

My conversation with Ivey ends on a down note, but I still have to finish the day. Next on my to-do list is to finish Bud's graphs. I contemplate the possible results, but I need to complete the graphs to prove my point. An hour and a half later, my proof is in front of me. The victims' common denominator is the competition cheerleading squad, high school, and I added modeling. I'll call Bud and Ivey and share the findings. Also, we need to add modeling to the search list. When the team reaches Tallahassee, I will ask Ivey to check with the tournament representatives to provide any records that might have given the killer the girls' names.

Lunch comes at just the right time today. I hustle out the back door and stop in the grocery store on my way home. Today would not be a good day to eat lunch in town because there are so many people around with too many questions. While eating lunch at my kitchen sink, I notice the house needs a good scrubbing, but then I remember the press release for Tonya lingers untouched. I schedule it for delivery at ten in the morning.

The afternoon flies by before I remember the press release again. Tomorrow's press conference will be short and sweet. I jot a few notes on a piece of paper, as I will release the only information I have on Tonya's discovery. The killer remains unknown, along with his whereabouts. Mr. Zon was supposed to call this morning to let me know about Tonya's funeral. I haven't heard from him yet. As much as I hate funerals, I will not miss Tonya's.

With no reason to stay at the office, I head home. My body needs rest, and I need clean clothes. As soon as I enter the house, I head straight for the laundry room and add clothes to the washer. Then I clean, starting with the bathrooms, then the bedroom, followed by the kitchen. Now, when Bud shows up, the house will be presentable.

My day ends as I complete my follow-up list for tomorrow. Every day it seems my list grows. I lay the list on my bedside table. Then, I rest my head on my pillow, thinking about the case and where it might lead.

Another sunny day jars me from a deep sleep. As I roll over to shield my eyes from the sun, my mind wanders to Bud. He didn't call last night, nor did Ivey. I waited for a phone call, just like I did as a high school student. The call never came. They are in the midst of their own investigation and are much closer to catching the killer than I am. So, I start my day with a hot shower and a cup of coffee.

Tons of messages greet me at the office. "Maggie, when did these come in? No one called my cell phone. So why, suddenly, does the press call?"

"I can't answer that, Sheriff. I'm not sure who told the press there would be a press conference today. Maybe it was an educated guess on their part." Maggie says as she shrugs her shoulders. I turn and head for my office, not liking the answer to my question.

Just because the press called this morning, I'm holding off the release. They can wait. It might be later in the afternoon or even in the morning. Sitting in my chair, I study the murder board again, even though I have memorized it. Cheerleading and modeling make the most sense. I sure hope the teams in Tallahassee come up with something. Maggie calls and advises Mr. Zon is holding on line one.

With unsteady hands and voice, I answer the call. Mr. Zon is short and curt, advising Tonya's funeral will be the day after tomorrow at eleven in the morning. They did not invite the public, but the sheriff's department is welcome. I thank him for the privilege and advise I will be there.

With the dreaded call complete, I decided to check out the warehouse again. The owner never returned my calls, and that makes me more suspicious. I call Taylor and Tuttle for back-up since the contents of the warehouse are unknown.

As I enter the lot, both deputies are already there. They park their vehicles on each side of the building, facing out. Law enforcement officers train to always face their vehicles outwards in case of a call. "Hey, guys, thanks for getting here so fast. I want to walk around the building again and to see if there are any changes."

Tuttle speaks first, "Sheriff, I think I have a different phone number for the owner, Stuart Milton Boards, than what you called earlier. Also, the document I found had the guy's first name spelled differently than the original. I spent time cross-referencing properties and owner contact information, and this information came from the deed records. Check this one against yours."

I pull out my notebook and find the number, "You are correct, Tuttle. Yours is different. Let me try the new number." Everyone waits as I dial the new number. The phone rings three times and then voicemail. "Still no answer. I left another message. However, this voice differed from the last, and neither message offered a name." I drop my phone into my pants pocket. Then I say, "Let's walk around the warehouse and look for changes since the last time we visited. Be sure to check the windows, doors, and tire tracks. We stay together. I don't want to take the chance of splitting up."

The first thing I notice is the box truck. It's still parked in the same area, and it is difficult to tell if someone moved the truck. Also, the warehouse appears vacant. The windows are so dirty you can't see inside. There are no other vehicles in the lot. However, when we turn the warehouse corner, there are visible tire tracks in the dirt. "Could one of you snap a picture of those tracks? The pictures might not be enough to get a make on the tires, but I'd like to try."

"The tire tracks prove someone was recently here. I don't recall seeing the tracks on the first visit. It hasn't rained since then, either." Taylor states.

"Agree, Taylor. I don't remember seeing them last time either. I want a warrant for the warehouse, but I need a legitimate reason. A judge will not sign one based on a woman's intuition." We walk back to our cars, and I place my hand on the handle as I say, "I'm going home. If you need me, call my cell. Thanks for coming out here."

Both deputy's wave as they enter their vehicles. I watch them check in with dispatch before leaving the lot. Glancing back at the warehouse, I still want to see what is inside. I can't stop my gut from feeling that something isn't right here.

With Bud and Ivey still away, I leave the office early and head home. I still haven't heard from Bud, and Taylor hasn't mentioned speaking with Ivey. I sit in my home office and pay bills and such while my mind ponders the case. Have these girls competed against each other? Or is there another reason they died together?

Nighttime is my hardest time and always has been. I wander through my house, trying to find an outlet for my stress. Typically, reading a book is how I end my day. Books are everywhere in my house. Tonight, a book isn't working because my mind travels to Bud and Ivey. Wonder what it would be like to be an FBI agent? Could I partner with Bud or Ivey? We work well together, but could two people have a relationship in our line of work and work together daily? You would literally spend every hour of every day together. Now, that is something to consider.

When morning comes, I am eager for the day with Bud and Ivey returning. Deputy Taylor and Tuttle are on standby for an update later in the morning. Sun shines through the lobby windows as I pass through. My office is clean and prepared for their return. I want their updates from Tallahassee and Alabama. It would be nice to deliver the news of the killer being captured to Tonya's parents before her funeral. I would hope that would provide some satisfaction.

A few hours later, Bud follows Ivey into my office. This case has tired both out, as I can see dark circles under their eyes. "Welcome back. The guys are on call for an update. Do you want to eat lunch first or update us on your adventure?"

Ivey answers without looking at Bud,

"We will do the update now. If you can't tell, we are exhausted. I'm going for a nap this afternoon if that is okay."

"Sure, it is. The rest will do your body good. I'm glad you're back. Freshen up, and I'll radio the guys to come to the office."

Fifteen minutes later, we sit around the office, and I introduce Deputy Brock Tuttle to Bud and Ivey. Bud and Ivey have heard mention of Tuttle, with no formal introduction until now. Then, I turn the floor over to Agent Ivey, and she starts, "I sent the video of the Mobile box truck to you, Sheriff. We will look at that in a moment. Lucy Monroe was a competition cheerleader, and a man promising her a modeling gig contacted her. Lucy's mom told her it was a fluke and begged her not to speak with this guy again. She thinks Lucy met him in Tallahassee, and the guy told Lucy she would be perfect in his magazine ad. Lucy's mom cannot describe the guy." Ivey looks at Bud, and then Bud takes over.

"We are searching online for the killer using the deceased victims' social media pages. I have added the words modeling and model to the search. Tallahassee seems to be the best place to catch this guy. The Alabama victims remain unidentified. The time spent in the water is making identification difficult. Does anyone have anything to add?"

"I want to ask the Tallahassee team to check with the tournament coordinators for a list of the cheerleader entries. They might list the girls' names under their respective high schools."

Bud grins, "I see where you are going with your train of thought. Nice work, Sheriff."

We spend the next two hours reviewing the information we have and updating anything new. The Mobile video doesn't add much to our evidence. With the picture being taken from a distance, the truck details are blurry. It looks similar to our box truck. But I can't guarantee it's the same. Finally, Ivey speaks up and states she is going to the hotel for a nap. Bud agrees and follows her out. I sit down at my desk and try to decide about the press release. The answer doesn't come, so I head home for a late lunch, hoping Bud will call me later.

Unsure of what to do with Bud and Ivey napping, I search my closet for something to wear to a funeral. My wardrobe comprises mostly uniforms and jeans. I don't have the in between clothes. Jeans are not appropriate for the county sheriff to wear to a funeral. So, I opt for a pressed and cleaned uniform. Funerals have always been hard for me throughout my life but especially since dad's death. However, I have every intention of attending Tonya's.

When I return to the office, Maggie meets me at the door with a grin on her face. "Hi, Maggie. Are you the bearer of good news?"

"I am, Sheriff. The word 'model' has shown up multiple times in the online searches for murder victims. It's a new lead!"

"That's great. It's about time something good happened for us. Are Agents Ivey and Bud here? We need to share the news."

"They haven't come back from their nap. You can give them the information."

"I will, Maggie. Thanks for the update."

The whiteboard needs a quick update. It is nice adding a note to our side of the board. The killer has a lengthy list on his side while our side is short. It will please Ivey and Bud. We can move forward with the Tallahassee team and expect results because the killer will be at the tournaments. That's his next stop on this horrific trail.

After work, I go home without a call from Ivey or Bud. They must be asleep, and that means another night wondering what is on Bud's mind. A squawking radio from dispatch greets me when I cross the threshold to the kitchen. "Dispatch, this is Sheriff Steele, come back."

"Sheriff, there is a report of a serious car accident in front of the hotel where our FBI friends are staying. Three cars and one entrapment per the caller." The dispatcher explains.

"Show me in route." I grab my keys and holster and head back to town. All I can think about are Bud and Ivey. Deputy Tuttle is on duty, so I radio him for an update.

"Sheriff to Tuttle," I repeat the same

message several times before I receive a response.

"Tuttle to Sheriff. I'm at the scene. The accident involves three vehicles. One local, two are from out of state. It appears the driver of the red car failed to yield on a left turn as they entered the traffic lanes from the hotel. The FBI agents are assisting with extrication."

"Be there in ten minutes. Sheriff, out."

The scene appears chaotic from a distance, but once I arrive, everything is running smoothly. An ambulance waits to take the entrapped victim to the hospital, and the fire department works to free the trapped while others stand by to mop up the scene. Bud and Ivey talk with Tuttle.

"Tuttle, can you give me a breakdown of the accident?" I ask while trying to concentrate on the accident instead of Bud.

"The red car with Tennessee tags turned left in front of the white truck with Georgia tags. The white truck clipped the back end of our local vehicle, driven by Mrs. Warren. She is not hurt. However, the passenger in the red car suffered significant injuries to their leg. The red car's driver appears disoriented, so they are getting a trip to the hospital, too. The driver of the white truck was alone and uninjured, although his truck is not drivable. There are multiple tow trucks on their way."

"Very thorough. Great job." After the accident, Bud and Ivey catch up with me and ask me to dinner with them and Taylor. I am exhausted, but I also want to see them, so we agree on a quick bite at the diner next door to the hotel.

Ivey describes their trip, and we discuss options about the team in Tallahassee since Maggie's news. "I can't believe we finally have a lead. The team recognizes the expectations are for them to capture the killer, and if they can't do that, then at least provide us with a viable suspect."

"Reminder for everyone, Tonya's funeral is tomorrow at eleven. They did not invite the press, and I confirmed our attendance, but only if you want to. Taylor and I are both going."

"I would like to go, but I am out of makeup. If you have some I can borrow, I'll go with you." Ivey states, then looks my way.

"Come to my house at around nine in the morning. That will be plenty of time to get to the funeral home." I don't keep a lot of makeup handy, but I do have a small stash tucked into a bathroom drawer.

We finish our hamburgers and bid each other a good night. Bud winks at me as he says, good night. I'm still eager to hear what is on his mind, but I guess I can wait one more day.

Chapter 11

Today is Tonya's funeral, and it will be a rough one. The weather is cooperating with sunshine but it's not helping my mood. What makeup I own sits on my bathroom counter, waiting for Agent Ivey. I add a little to my face, hoping it will help my attitude. It doesn't. With my uniform on, I wear my hair up in a ponytail.

As I finish dressing, Maggie calls to update me on last night's action. Thankfully, not a lot happened in the county after Tuttle cleared the accident. The passenger survived their injuries, but they had to endure three hours of surgery rebuilding the mangled leg. I remind Maggie today is Tonya's funeral, and I won't be in the office until late afternoon.

While waiting for Ivey, I ponder my relationship with Bud. We seem to get along okay, but we haven't spent enough time alone to have any deep conversations about life and each other's dreams. There is no sense thinking about a relationship if our dreams collide. Our careers will be hard enough to combat.

Someone knocks on my front door, and it better be Agent Ivey. The press will not be welcome in my life today. "Good morning, Agent Ivey. Come in."

"Thanks, Sheriff. I appreciate you letting me borrow some makeup. I'll try to get to the store at some point."

"No problem. Can I offer you coffee?" I watch Ivey as she zeroes in on my family pictures. She shakes her head from side to side, I suppose as an answer to my question. Since Dad's death, I catch myself staring at the photos and remembering every place we took them.

"Is this your dad in the picture? How old were you?" Agent Ivey asks.

"Yes. That's Dad and me at the lake. I'm not sure how old I was there. Let me look at the back of the picture. He always wrote the date and the location on every picture." Ivey hands the picture frame to me, and the photo slides out of its holder. When the picture turns over, my breath catches in my throat. My dad's and Agent Ivey's handwriting closely match. Glancing at Ivey, she doesn't understand why I am faltering at her questions. "I was eight in that picture." So many questions run through my mind, I don't know what to do. I want to ask her questions about her childhood, but I'm not sure how.

"It's a pleasant picture, and it looks like you had fun. Show me the way to your makeup. We don't want to be late," Agent Ivey states while looking around the room.

I carefully slide the photo back into the frame and place it in the same position when another knock on the front door disrupts my thoughts. When I open the door, I say, "Hi Taylor, I didn't expect you by here this morning. Everything okay?"

"Yes, Sheriff. It's fine. Bud told me Ivey is here, and I am looking for a little time to talk with her before the funeral. Do you mind if I come in?"

"You are welcome anytime. Did you bring Bud with you?" I ask with a little too much hope in my voice.

"Look outside for yourself," Taylor replies with a grin on his face.

I can't believe it. Here I am concerned because Bud hasn't called, and he shows up with Taylor. Bud leans on Taylor's car with his arms crossed. He waves at me when I peer around the door. I wave back and step inside to retrieve my things.

I push the ideas regarding Ivey to the back burner as Bud rides with me, and Ivey jumps in the car with Taylor to go to Tonya's funeral. We enjoy small talk on the way to the funeral home. I share with Bud about my reluctance to attend funerals. "I've got your six, Sheriff. If it gets too hard on you, give me a sign. I'll make sure you exit without drawing attention."

"Aw, Bud. Thank you for going with me, even though you don't have to. I appreciate it." I reach over and rub his arm.

"Sheriff, I will be there for you. Remember, we still need to talk, and I want it to happen today."

I turn my eyes back to the road ahead.

Bud is serious about his talk with me. All I can hope is he is not leaving me. The case remains open, so I hope he will at least stay until its conclusion.

We arrive at the funeral in tandem. I park at the end of the lot and back the car into a parking space because we are always ready, and Taylor does the same. The lot is half full of cars already with even more entering. When the clock strikes 10:55 am, we enter the funeral home. We survey the attendees to see if anyone unusual has shown up for the service. Tonya's parents sit in the front row of the chapel, along with other family members. Mr. Zon nods as his stare meets my eye when we enter the chapel. The chapel is gorgeous, boasting stained glass windows and flowers everywhere. Tonya liked purple roses, and her parents had her chrome-colored casket covered in purple roses. It is a breathtaking sight.

The service starts on time. People deliver kind words about Tonya. Her cousin makes a solemn statement, and then Darlene adds a few comments. Tonya would be proud to hear how much her family and friends loved her. I glance around the chapel and don't see a soul who doesn't belong. Either the killer isn't aware of the funeral or just doesn't care enough to attend her service.

After the service, we are the first two cars to leave the lot. I can't go to the graveside. My insides are twisted, having to endure the funeral service. We leave the graveside to the family, and we return to the sheriff's office to discuss the Tallahassee team.

Messages and sticky notes cover my desk, reminding me of tasks again. My face turns red when I read the sticky note taped to the phone. "I can't believe I didn't follow up on the press release. We never had a press conference after they found Tonya's body. How did I forget something like that?"

"It was a smart call if you ask me. Let the family bury their daughter in peace. Schedule a press conference for four this afternoon. That gives us plenty of time to write a release. You're not saying a lot, anyway. You'll be fine." Bud says reassuringly.

"Sounds like a plan. You have a way of calming me and making situations sound logical." I notify Maggie of our upcoming press release. She can make notifications for the department.

"Grab your pen, Sheriff. The writing begins."

Twenty minutes later, our rough outline of the next press release is complete. "Now, that wasn't so bad, was it, Sheriff?" Bud asks.

"No, it wasn't so bad. It is the thought of having to do it, that's all. Now, to give the update without shedding tears over Tonya will be difficult. We wanted to find her alive, but it wasn't in the cards. I want to see this killer behind bars because I want to ask him a few questions."

"Once we capture him, I'll make sure you get time with him. You won't see him alone, but you will see him. You deserve that after all that has happened here."

I can't seem to get words out, so I shake my head in acknowledgment. Grabbing the phone, I call the bullpen for Taylor and Ivey. We need to make headway on the Tallahassee team. They are leaving tomorrow to set up the areas for surveillance.

Taylor and Ivey enter the office with expectant looks on their faces. "What's up, Sheriff? Are we ready to work on the team assignments?"

"Yes, we need to get a handle on the staff plans. Maggie scheduled the press release for four this afternoon, so only a couple of hours remain."

Ivey says, "Then let's do it. I have the list of agents going with us to Tallahassee."

"Going with us? Does that mean you two are leaving again?" I ask with a curt tone in my voice. Today has already been stressful, now Ivey slips in, and she and Bud are leaving again. I can't seem to keep my emotions in control. There is too much happening in my life. I don't want them to go, even if it is their job. Times like these are when I question a relationship with another law enforcement person.

"Bud, you didn't tell her?" Ivey questions him with a scowl.

"No, I didn't yet. We are having dinner tonight, and I thought we would discuss it then. Thanks for the slip, Ivey." Bud states as he fumes at the debacle.

"Sorry, Sheriff. Bud and I are leaving first thing in the morning for Tallahassee. We are the lead agents for the Tallahassee team. You are on the list for any updates that come out of there. The competition starts tomorrow afternoon, and we need to set it up before the start. We are coming back here when the competition ends in four days."

"Somehow, I knew you would go. I guess I didn't realize it would be tomorrow. Let's see your teams, and we can make the assignments quickly with all of us helping."

Based on the list from Ivey, there will be twenty-four agents involved in Team Tallahassee. We assign each agent a partner with a particular task. Some agents are outside surveillance and some inside. Other agents will be concession stand workers, inside security personnel, and administration participants. Once we make the team assignments, we make a list of items needed to complete this assignment. Ivey and Bud work their phones to make sure everything will be in place tomorrow.

Next on the list is the press release. While Bud and Ivey complete their duties with the Tallahassee team, I deliver the press release. I divulge no information to the press that could jeopardize our case against the killer if we need it. I only accept three questions at the end of the release, and I quickly answer them. Breathing a sigh of relief, I walk back into my office, sink into my chair, and lay my head back on it.

With my eyes closed and my head laid back on my chair, I feel someone standing at my door. I don't want to open my eyes because someone will ask me to do something. Today has been difficult, but I can say I've made it this far.

"Sheriff, are you okay?" Bud asks with a tinge of concern in his voice.

"Yeah. I'm fine. Just a long day, and I have to admit I am glad it's almost over."

"Well, it's not exactly over," Bud says with a grin.

"What do you mean by that? What's happened now?"

"Nothing has happened, but you promised me supper, remember? I'm here to collect on that promise."

"There is no way I forgot that promise. I thought you might be too tired, especially since you are leaving in the morning for Tallahassee." I counter.

Bud grins as he says, "You're not talking me out of it. Grab your things."

"Oh no, you don't. I'm going home to change clothes into something besides a uniform. Want me to pick you up?"

"Nope. I'm riding along with you. You are not getting out of my sight, Sheriff."

"Well, then. Let's get a move on."

As we leave the building, I inform dispatch to reach me by cell phone for emergencies. Bud has his hand on my elbow again, and it feels just as good as the last time. In the car, I feel awkward, not knowing what to talk about. I make small talk until we arrive at my house, then I escape to my bedroom. Closing the bedroom door gives me relief from the outside. Bud has my nerves working overtime because I have not a clue what he wants to discuss. I take a quick shower and throw on clean clothes. As I look in the mirror, I question if Bud has ever seen me in street clothes. His expression will answer the question.

As I open the bedroom door, I take a deep breath, trying to relax and enjoy my time with Bud because I suspect he won't be around long. The FBI has him traveling to different states at a moment's notice. Bud waits in the family room. He stands when he hears me walking down the hall. As I enter the room, he turns, and his lip's part.

"You look good in a uniform, but good grief, girl. You look terrific in street clothes." Bud's grin spreads from one side of his face to the other. He walks over and hugs me. It is our first hug since meeting each other, and we fit like a glove.

"Thank you for the compliment, Bud. You know how to make a girl feel good."

"Follow me, Jada, or should I keep

calling you Sheriff?" Bud asks.

"Jada sounds nice. I don't hear it often."

Bud reaches out and takes my hand, and we walk out to the car. He drives to the restaurant, the only one in town to serve a decent steak. We talk little as I listen to the radio squawk, and Bud glances over at me. As we are getting out of the car, our eyes meet over the top of the vehicle, and it catches us with a surge of feelings we don't expect.

"Smells good out here. I hope the place isn't so crowded that we can't enjoy a quiet conversation." Bud eyes the parking lot and notices it is half full.

"I'll get us a table in the back away from the families. They usually sit me back there anyway, in case I get called away, I can go through the kitchen and exit the back door."

The owner handles my request with grace, and my favorite table is available, so we take it. We both order steaks, baked potatoes, and salads. Then Bud gets down to business.

"You listen while I talk. Don't interrupt until I say everything on my mind, and then it's your turn. Okay?" Bud asks.

"Ok, Bud. I'll try not to interrupt." My hands are under the table, so he cannot see them shake. I haven't been this nervous with a guy since college.

Bud bows his head and takes a deep breath before he speaks. "Sheriff, Jada, I like you a lot. I felt the pull the moment I saw you.

At first sight, love is not something I believe in or have ever thought about, but I found it if it is true. Marriage has never been on my radar because of my job. I'm not asking you to marry me yet, but it is not off the table either. I want to spend more time with you, away from our jobs, and if we both feel the same way, then I would like to see if we can make our relationship work. I would never ask you to give up your job because I would make a move with the FBI or do something different. We'll make adjustments on the job issue when we reach that point."

I sit there in awe. Flabbergasted is the word that pops into my mind. I like Bud, but I expected nothing like this so soon. My face is beet red by the time Bud finishes his spiel. I have a hard time conjuring up the words, so I stammer through a response.

"Bud, I told you earlier that you know how to make a girl feel good. You blew me away. I have been anxious about your talk because I thought you were telling me you are leaving and returning to Louisiana. You can't imagine how happy this makes me. I would love the opportunity to see if we can make our relationship work. Louisiana to Georgia is quite the trip, but we can worry about that later. How about taking a vacation? We could put together a beach trip after we solve the case if you are up for it."

"Do you mean it, Jada? Do you want to try it? It has scared me to mention it. You know how it is in law enforcement. If you are not in it, it's hard to understand the commitment."

"Yes, Bud. If I could lean across the table and kiss you, I would. But with the families in the restaurant, I don't think that would be appropriate for the little kids." I wink at him as I say the word kiss.

"You wait until we get out of here. I'm taking you up on your offer of a kiss. Here's our food, eat quickly, please. I'm tired of waiting to be alone, and tomorrow will be here before we are ready."

Supper flies by after the initial conversation. I am not on pins and needles any longer now that the relationship talk is over. Time spent with Bud is the most enjoyable. We clean our dinner plates, and Bud pays the tab when Agent Ivey and Deputy Taylor walk up to our table. As much as I like them, I don't want to share Bud tonight.

"Hey, guys. Are you coming or going?" I ask them, hoping they are just arriving.

Taylor answers for the duo, "We are just getting here for supper. We are running a little late tonight."

I watch as Taylor squeezes Ivey's hip, which brings her a little closer to him. Trying not to make too much about it, I peek at Bud, and he winks at me. "We have finished our meal. The table is yours if you want it."

"We will take it. I wondered who they had sitting at this table. It shouldn't be a surprise that it's you, Sheriff. This is your favorite."

Bud and I leave the two at our table. "I sure was glad they didn't ask us to go somewhere with them. I do not want to share you with anyone tonight."

When I glance over my shoulder at Bud, I say, "I've had no one read my mind before, but I thought the same thing about sharing you."

He reaches out and takes my hand, and we walk hand-in-hand to the car. Bud drives us to my house, and he never let's go of my hand. Tonight is the best night I have had in a long time. Unfortunately, tomorrow this will only be a memory but a sweet one at that.

The rest of the night progresses in a blur. The happiest of times are always when the clock moves in a hurry. Before we know it, morning comes, and morning means Bud leaves for Tallahassee. On the flip side, it also means the sooner he and Ivey get to Tallahassee and find the killer, the faster they return. We enjoy coffee together before we meet with Ivey and Taylor at the office. "So, Sheriff, how are you going to explain it to the troops when I get out of your car at the office?" Bud smiles a wicked grin.

"There is no need to explain anything. I'm grown, and my life choices are mine to make. Now, Maggie might be a little concerned. She watches my back, so I don't get hurt."

"I'll take care of Maggie. She will understand exactly how I feel and that I carry no intention of hurting you in any way. How does that sound?"

"Sounds like you have it all figured out, sir. We need to get going."

Bud hugs me as no one has ever hugged me before. I can't tell if he hugs me like this, just if he never gets the chance again, or if he really loves me. I don't push him away to ask. It feels too good.

The drive to the office is slow. If I admit it myself, I am not ready to see him leave, even if only for a few days. "Bud, I have a stupid question. Are you are coming back here after Tallahassee?" I glance at his face waiting for an answer.

"Yes. I promise I will come back here to you, and we will be in constant contact, too. Keep your cell phone handy. I'll call that number instead of the office phone."

"Okay. I can do that. Sorry to sound like a sniveling kid, but you're mine. I'm not willing to let you go." I confess.

"Oh, Sheriff, I like the sound of that. I'll keep that in the back of my brain while I'm away. It will give me something to hold on to, too. I'm banking on catching this guy and coming back here in the next couple of days."

I enter the lot and park at the back door. Taylor's car is already here. When I see it, it makes me wonder how their night was last night. There is no way it was as good as ours. Bud sees me looking at Taylor's car. "Do you think Taylor and Ivey found love as we did?

That would be something, huh?"
   "I think so, Bud."

Chapter 12

All eyes are on us when we walk into the bullpen. I'm not sure if the group is expecting an announcement, but they don't get one. "Overnight status, Tuttle, my office."

Tuttle trots into my office with papers in hand. "Sheriff, the only report from last night was a man walking alongside the road where the fire occurred. The caller stated the man appeared to be looking for something. He was scraping his foot in the fire area, picking debris up in his hand, and then throwing it back down. The man's description is vague. He appears to be around six feet, 150-180 pounds, wearing work boots, hair color unknown. A knit cap covered his hair."

"Tuttle, check-in with Sal. Let's see if he stopped in the store for anything. If you are not on duty today, send someone else to handle it. You need to take a break."

"Ok, Sheriff. I'll check the duty roster."

"Maggie, anything on the overnight shift for me?"

"The only call we received was the guy walking in the fire area. No other reports."

Now that I've relieved the overnight shift, I join Bud and Ivey in the adjoining room. They plan to leave in the next few minutes, and my insides tighten at the thought. Sitting at the table are people I care deeply for, two of which are leaving shortly. I suck in my breath and sit alongside Taylor. Ivey discusses the plans we have been working on for a few days now. "Sheriff, would you take a minute and read over these one last time? We don't want to miss anything."

I stammer and answer a squeaky, "Sure." My eyes are on the papers, but I can't comprehend anything. So, I play the part and hand them back to Ivey. "I can't think of anything else. Only if something happens in Tallahassee, be ready to change plans."

An hour later, I stand in the sheriff's office parking lot and watch Bud and Ivey leave for Tallahassee. My heart lodges in my throat, as this trip will be dangerous for the entire team. Once the killer is aware, the police are after him; who knows what he will do to protect himself?

With Bud and Ivey on their way to Florida, I decide to catch up on my county work and backtrack to the arson case in the woods. Maybe Taylor or Tuttle feel like taking a walk in some smoke-filled woods this afternoon. "Taylor, are you in the bullpen?"

Three seconds later, I hear, "Yes, Sheriff. I am." Taylor responds as background noise interferes.

"What was that noise?" I question, wondering what I am missing.

"That was Tuttle saying he is still in the

bullpen too," Taylor states with a chuckle.

"Could both of you come to see me?" As I return the phone to my desk, I see Tonya's warrant information sitting in my email.

Something bumps my office door, and when I look up, two grown men are trying to enter my door at the same time. "What in the world? That door isn't big enough for the both of you at the same time." I say while chuckling. "Take a seat while Tuttle is still here. I want an update on the warehouse owner and a follow-up on any additional information from the fire. I also received the information on Tonya's cell phone calls. Then, Tuttle, you are off the clock for a while. Any other items of interest?"

Tuttle clears his throat and begins first. "The owner of the warehouse, Stuart Milton Boards, has returned none of my voicemails. I rode by the warehouse last night while I was on duty, and nothing has changed. It is still dark. The box truck remains parked in the same general area. I snapped a few pictures showing where they parked the box truck. The photos will help me determine if the truck moves."

"Who is the owner of the warehouse, and is he local? I don't recognize that name."

"No, Sheriff, he lists his address in Pervis, Mississippi. The number I call goes straight to voicemail."

"Give me the address, and I'll chat with the Sheriff of whatever county that is."

"Lamar County, Sheriff."

"Great. Thanks, I'll check on that this afternoon. Taylor, any updates on the fire?"

"Nothing from the DNR, Sheriff. It doesn't sound like they are too interested in it. Too many acres to cover seeing how it is fire season, and they are short-handed."

"That's what I thought. I will make another trip through the burned section of the woods. If either of you feels like a walk, you are welcome to join. I'm planning on an afternoon walk around three."

I clicked the email open and read the results. They were not pleasing but expected. I share with the guys the killer communicated with Tonya with a burner phone. There is no way to trace it, but the technician is searching the barcode for where he purchased the phone.

The news was another disappointment, but both deputies stand up and tell me they will see me at three. These guys are so funny. They stay in constant competition with one another. Heaven forbid one gets asked to do something, and I leave the other one out.

The sheriff of Lamar County, Mississippi, explains our warehouse owner is in the import-export business, and he is an influential member of the county. The owner has several warehouses in his area and other states. It perturbs me he doesn't offer to help find the owner so I can speak with him. "Sheriff, do you have contact information for this person? His warehouse is the subject of a murder investigation in my county, and he's not responded to voicemails."

"You don't mean it? I'll see what I can find it and get back to you." As I hang up on the sheriff of Lamar County, a lousy sensation creeps through my soul.

I add my conversation to the murder board. I do not recall ever speaking with a more disinterested sheriff in all my years. He acts as if he does not care about the murder or the owner of the warehouse. Wonder how much money the warehouse owner donated to the sheriff's campaign during the last election? The word murder typically gets law enforcement officers to react, not merely saying they will get back to you.

While I stand at the board, I review the notes from the fire. There isn't much to go on, but it deserves another search. I am not ready to let it go. The fire is a crucial part of Tonya's death, and we haven't found the key yet. Looking at the clock, I still have a while before meeting the guys to walk the burned woods.

My desk phone rings, and I answer a call from the crime scene tech. It delights me that he has uncovered a partial fingerprint from the candy wrapper Taylor found in the woods. Even though the fingerprint isn't enough to run through AFIS, we can use it later. It will place the killer in the woods.

After my conversation with the crime scene tech, I spend the next few hours returning messages, writing notes, and adding information to the murder board. Every time I review the board, I fall back to the cheerleading competition. The method of contact remains a mystery.

Maggie graces the door to my office. "Got a minute, Sheriff?"

"Come on in, Maggie. What's up?"

"I have a few messages from the press. Several of the national networks are arriving in town as we speak. They want an update from you and your team." She grimaces as she awaits my answer.

"I can't provide an update right now. The team is setting up in Tallahassee, and I am going back to the woods to search for evidence surrounding Tonya's death. Leave the messages with me, and I'll handle them. Are you doing okay, Maggie?"

"I'm sad about Tonya, and I'm ready for this case to be over. Our lives have not been the same since the kids found those bodies in the ditch. But I think something good is coming out of this horror." Maggie grins at me as she says the last part.

"What are you talking about?" I ask, trying to hide my smile.

"Is it true you and Bud are in a relationship now? And, what about Agent Ivey and Deputy Taylor?"

"Yes, we are in a relationship, or I should say we are going to give it a try and see if it works with our careers and the distance between us. Taylor hasn't confessed his love for Ivey yet, even though I suspect it's coming."

"Oh, Sheriff, that is great. I am so happy for you. As the old saying goes, love shows up when you least expect it. You two make an impressive pair. You'll find a way to make it work."

"Thanks, Maggie. I appreciate your support. We haven't had time for our talks, with this case taking up my time. Once it's closed, we can get back to normal. Hang in there for a little while longer."

"I will. Your hiking buddies are here. I'll leave you all to make the trip to the woods. Be careful." Maggie turns and walks away from the office with her shoulders slumped. Something is bothering her, and it is more than the case.

"Grab your gear. Meet you at the car in ten minutes." I say to the guys as I stop by dispatch. With all that happened this morning, I didn't stop by for my daily visit.

In Taylor's vehicle, we return to the woods fire when Taylor glances at me and says, "Sheriff, I don't want to pry, but something is going on with Maggie. She has been acting strange. I asked her about it, and she blamed it on the case."

"Maggie acted upset before we left, but she didn't elaborate. I'll talk to her and see if I can get an answer." Thinking back on my conversations with Maggie, she has mentioned no issues with the staff or personally. When we garner a moment, I'll approach her and see if she will tell me.

The crime scene tape is still in place, bringing back the images of Tonya's body. My body shudders, thinking about that day. I am looking for a logical reason for her body to be in these burned woods. It still makes little sense. There are no houses out here, no roads, other than fire roads.

"Sheriff, are you ready?" Tuttle leans over the seat to face me.

"I believe so. Let's go searching. However, we need to stay together, at least close enough to see each other. With the killer still on the loose, we don't know what to expect." I inform the men as best I can without giving away my uneasiness about the situation.

We march into the woods with me in the middle. Our hands rest on our holsters, always at the ready—an hour into the hike, and nothing to show for our time. "Talk me through this. Why or how did Tonya show up here? Was the killer hiding out in the woods, or did they leave Tonya here as a ploy?"

Both deputies rationalize an answer. "I think they were hiding here, maybe in a tent or something. Although we found no evidence of a tent unless he took it, or it burned."

Tuttle counters, "My guess is the killer had a tent where he kept Tonya. He got scared when we searched the area because we worried him—he was scared we might walk upon them. He kills Tonya, takes the tent, and leaves on a four-wheeler out the back. That's the only way I can see him getting out of the woods without being seen."

Both scenarios are on point. "You're right, guys. The tent and four-wheeler sound most logical. That explains why we can't find anything usable out here. Although, I'd like to take a quick walk on the other side of the creek where Tonya's body was located. He left in that direction. Was she running toward him or away from him at the time he shot her?"

"Surely she wasn't running toward the killer. Unless he was taunting her about saving her from the fire." Taylor adds while looking at the murder scene. "I hope I am the one to capture the killer, dead or alive," he continues.

"Now, I want none of you killing anyone. Taking a person's life is a serious business. You will endure scrutiny from the GBI, fill out tons of reports, answer a gazillion questions, and last but not least, it stays with you forever." I explain as I try to keep a blank face.

The deputies stare at me as if they are waiting on me to continue. There is no need to share why and how I know that. Just suffice it to say, I experienced firsthand how it feels to kill someone in the line of duty.

We walk about a hundred yards beyond the creek and come upon a clearing. A bunch of tall green plants grows in long, straight lines. I can't fathom how many plants this might be. The clearing isn't large, but someone has covered it in plants. The guys look at me with their mouths open.

"Is this what I think it is? Someone is growing marijuana in our county. Take photos from all sides. I'll call ATF and ask them to do a flyover. The plot might be too small for them. If so, we'll see if the Corps of Engineers wants it. If not, it's ours. However, we won't touch it until we solve Tonya's case. Don't get too close to it. I've heard growers use snakes to keep people out of their patches."

"That's all you need to say, Sheriff. Ready to head back now? I've seen enough." Tuttle turns and walks back without waiting for us.

"Taylor, I think we know what scares Tuttle!" I shout.

"Tuttle, are you going to let a little snake scare you off?" Taylor asks with a chuckle.

"Even men fear snakes. Yes, I fear snakes unless you want me to pump them full of bullet holes. See you two back at the car." Tuttle explains.

"Wait up, Tuttle. We are going back with you." I try to appease him. We don't need him to be hot and bothered over a little ribbing. "Let's add marijuana to our murder board. The killer might have used the fire to protect the grow plot. Maybe the fire was a diversion."

160

Taylor pauses, then adds, "It might not be the killer's plants. It might be a local person growing and selling, and the killer stumbled on it by accident. There is no evidence pointing to the killer growing this weed."

"You're right, Taylor. I'm trying to connect everything to this guy. I'll make the calls and see what happens with the plot. Hopefully, another agency will take it. We have a heavy enough workload with this murder case."

We walk back in silence. It is nice to have a moment to myself, even if guys surround me. The car is waiting for us when we clear the wood line. Our radio squawks as Taylor opens the door. He replies to dispatch.

"Sheriff, dispatch has a phone message for you. They want you to call them."

"Great. Now what?" I step to the back of the car, so I can put my things in the trunk before calling them. Dispatch reports Bud is trying to reach me, but my phone wasn't working. "Bud was trying to find me while we were walking. Apparently, we were out of range. I'll call him later." I share the message from dispatch because it feels good knowing someone is checking on me.

The office is empty when we enter. Even Maggie left a few minutes early. I walk into my office and sit down at my desk. There are no messages for me, which is unusual. I pluck my phone from my pocket and dial Bud. He answers on the second ring, and we chat about Tallahassee and the team. Everything seems to be going as planned. Team members have their assignments. The surveillance pair started their shift a few hours ago. They will watch the auditorium. I share my afternoon in the woods and the marijuana plot. Bud agrees with the guys that the field probably belongs to a local person, and then I let him ramble for a few minutes. Then I tell him I am going home. He ends the call by saying he will talk with me later this evening. My heart rate kicks up—two phone calls in one day.

Before leaving for the day, I make the necessary calls to the ATF regarding the plot field. They will inspect it and get back to me tomorrow. I draw a line through this call and move the follow-up to tomorrow.

Once home, the smoky smell I wear has to go, so I jump into a scorching hot shower. Then, supper is up next. Nothing appeals to my taste buds, so popcorn won the war. I keep looking around like something is missing. Bud is the missing part. It isn't long before my phone rings, and Bud and I enjoy a friendly conversation about us. Nothing to do about work for either of us. We discuss trips we would like to take together. All in all, it is a great conversation to end the day, and it relaxes me enough so I can sleep.

The next morning, I awake to bright sunshine with a touch of a breeze but still hot.

Bud already sent text updates early this morning with nothing to report. They are all set up at their stations. Today is the first day of the competition, and Bud said he has never seen so many young girls in one place in his life.

At the office, my goal is to find out what is bothering Maggie. I can't lose her. She is my rock. "Maggie, can you come into my office? Shut the door, please."

Maggie sits in a chair across from my desk, and when I see her, she looks like she is about to burst into tears. "What's wrong, Maggie? Don't ignore me because I can tell something is up."

Tears pour out of her eyes. "Sheriff, I don't want you to move away with Bud. I love my job, and I can't work for anyone but you." Maggie's words rush out of her mouth.

"Whoa, Maggie. Where did the idea of me moving come from? I'm not moving anywhere. We will try to have a relationship, but how we do that is up in the air. I'm not giving up my job, and neither is he." I walk around the desk to face Maggie. "Why didn't you come to me with your concerns? I thought we were closer than this."

Maggie sniffs and wipes the tears from her face as she states, "You are so busy. I couldn't interrupt the case because it requires so much of our time, and I knew you would come to see me when you had the time. I should have been able to work through it on my own."

"Thanks for telling me, Maggie. I thought you were leaving me. Now that our discussion is behind us, are there any messages from yesterday afternoon? There weren't any on my desk when I returned from the woods."

"Just the one from Bud. Thanks, Sheriff." Maggie exits the office with a skip in her step.

At least I made one person happy today. Now, I can only hope the rest of the day is as pleasant. I walk down the hall to the jail to check on things there. Our building also houses the county jail, and it is under my control. We hold between seventy-five and one hundred inmates, county and federal, at any one time. The captain of the jail division is Eric Grayson. He's worked at the sheriff's office for as long as I care to remember. He worked for my dad. There is never trouble from the jail division unless we house an unruly inmate. Captain Grayson keeps it running smoothly, mostly. I have just finished my conversation with Grayson when Maggie pages me over the radio system. Her voice alerts me to trouble.

I make record time reaching the other side of the compound. "Maggie, what's up?"

"Sheriff, Bud is holding, and he says it's urgent." Maggie blurts out.

Chapter 13

As I grab the phone, sirens blare in the background, and my heart lands in my stomach. I sit down, waiting for the update. "Sheriff, sorry for the sirens, but we added troops since we have a missing girl from the cheerleading competition. Tori Slack told her friend she was meeting a guy about a modeling opportunity, and these opportunities don't happen often, and she would not miss out. Her friend mentioned Tori talks about being a model all the time. Ivey already notified the Tallahassee sheriff of the possible box truck connection, and they issued a BOLO. I want you and your guys to be on alert in case he comes back to your area."

"Bud, I can't believe this. Where was she when she vanished?" I jot notes as Bud continues.

"That's the hard part. We are not sure because Tori was scheduled to cheer in the third group. They didn't notify us of Tori's disappearance until after their performance. The chaperone thought Tori might be sick and went back to the room. They checked, and she wasn't there. They brought us in at that point. Of course, it was hours after she left. The video in the hotel doesn't show Tori entering today. It shows the group leaving this morning, and we spotted Tori walking in the middle of the group with friends, but that's the last time we caught her on camera."

"Where does she live? Is it another out-of-state girl?" I question, trying to glean as much information as time would allow.

"Tori lives in West Palm Beach, and Ivey spoke with her parents earlier. They are on their way to Tallahassee as we speak. They had no idea about Tori meeting with someone about a modeling gig. Tori talks about her idea of modeling, but the family hasn't pursued it. They assumed it was a passing phase. Tori has a lot of ideas of what she wants to be when she grows up."

"Some phase. Were Tori's friends aware of the modeling opportunity?"

"Her friend is with the police now sharing what she knows. Ivey is with her. We are setting up teams to begin the search around the auditorium. You and I realize that will be fruitless. This guy has taken her away from here to a place unknown. Sorry to rush, but I need to run. I'll call you tonight. Be safe."

"You too," I say to a dial tone.

"Maggie, call Taylor, Tuttle, and Johnson for an immediate meeting in my office."

While I wait for the deputies to arrive, my mind flies in a thousand directions. Now, the killer has taken a girl from a cheerleading competition with tons of people around. How did he do it with no one seeing him? Is he part of the tournament or auditorium staff? He must mingle with the girls somehow, strike up a conversation, tell them what they want to hear, set a meeting time and place, and then poof. The girls vanish without a trace.

"Sheriff? Are you ready for us?" Johnson inquires as he watches me ponder the latest news.

"Sorry, my mind is wandering. Bud called with an update from Tallahassee, and it's not good. Take a seat, if you want, but I'll make it short. Bud advised the killer took a girl from the cheerleading competition about four hours ago. The missing girl is Tori Slack. She lives with her parents in West Palm Beach, Florida. Tori's parents are on their way to Tallahassee. They issued a BOLO for the box truck we think the killer is using for his abductions. Bud suggests we remain vigilant in case the guy comes back to our area. I want one of you to ride out to the warehouse and ensure that the truck we've seen there is still parked there. If not, call me. We will monitor all roads in and out of the county. Granted, we cannot cover every road, but roving lookouts work, too. Questions?"

Taylor asks, "Have they provided us with a photo of the girl?"

"Not yet. Bud and Ivey are working on that now. I'll send it to your phones once I receive it."

Next, Tuttle asks, "Want us to let the air

out of the tires of the box truck at the warehouse? It will slow the guy down if he uses it." He shrugs his shoulders as he offers the suggestion.

"Do it. Be careful. Change of plans—you both go to the warehouse together. Call me with the outcome. That's it. Johnson, I'd like you to cruise Shallow Bottoms."

The deputies make a mad dash for the door. I listen as their cars peel out of the parking lot one by one. At least they don't turn on the lights and sirens as that would draw unnecessary attention. Attention is not what we need right now. The press will drive us crazy when they get a hold of this latest revelation.

"Sheriff, everything okay? Bud sounds upset." Maggie asks through the door.

I recount the Tallahassee incident to Maggie, including the BOLO on the box truck. Maggie is my first line of defense when events occur. She handles the phone calls and needs any updated information on what is happening. But her expression tells me I made a mistake by sharing too much information. She also takes this stuff to heart.

Maggie's eyes are enormous as she looks at me and says, "I shouldn't be prying. I didn't realize it was about the case. Bud sounded in a hurry, but I assumed it was because he wanted to talk with you personally. That poor girl, alone with that guy. I hope the parents can help find her." Then Maggie turns around and escapes quickly.

Back at the murder board, I add another missing girl, and I jot an idea down, too. Bud and Ivey need to check with the tournament officials about unfamiliar people volunteering their time to help at the competition. Maybe the guy has weaseled himself into the mix of workers. He could have disguised himself as a concession stand worker, janitor, or greeter with little difficulty.

My cell phone rings. I answer on the half-ring, "Sheriff Steele."

"Sheriff, Taylor. We are at the warehouse, and the truck is still here, but by appearance, it has recently moved. There are drag marks at the back. Something was loaded or unloaded at this location. However, the building is secured. There are no lights or signs of life anywhere. We walked the perimeter, and even the light in the back is out."

"Ok. Is the hood of the truck cold or hot?"

"Hold on, Sheriff." I hear him walking on gravel over to the truck. "It's cold."

"Deflate a tire and start your roving patrols. I've notified the surrounding cities, too."

"10-4 Sheriff." Deputy Taylor signs off.

The owner of the warehouse is into importing and exporting items. Could that be people? But the killer murdered the girls he took, so he is not selling them for sex. He uses them for himself, then kills and dumps them. No one can determine how long these girls stay alive once taken, but the thought of that poor girl with this monster makes me sick to my stomach.

I've done all I can today. Maggie is calmer for now. The box truck has a flat tire. Bud and his team are knee-deep in a mess with a missing girl. Time to go home.

I lie in bed with horrible images running through my mind, unable to conjure up sleep. Along with the images, the fact Bud never called me has me unsettled. No one calls with updates, so I am assuming nothing else transpired after Tori. That can mean one thing: no new leads. However, tomorrow is another day.

The sheriff's office is peaceful upon my arrival the following day as it is bright and early before shift change. I gave up on sleep and came into the office early. The job always keeps me occupied. Today, of all days, it is budget items. The budget is my least liked portion of my duties, and two hours into the budget, the office phone rings. Maggie isn't in yet, so I answer it.

"Hi, Bud. You sound exhausted. Are you okay? You called my office line."

"Sorry. I thought I touched your cell phone number. I'm fine, but with Tori missing, there wasn't much sleep last night. Knowing you, you slept a little too. There are no updates and no witnesses who saw Tori leaving with a guy. The second day of the competition starts in one hour. The teams are in place. Ivey met with the tournament coordinator about new people helping, and nothing came from that either. Our surveillance plan changed a tad. Most agents walk the hallways and concession areas while Ivey and another female agent work the staging areas. If any fresh ideas come to you, share them. We are at a loss."

"Do the volunteers wear photo ID name tags?" I question.

"Yes, and they were all signed out by the correct owners. Although we know, that doesn't always mean the correct person is wearing it. Good idea. We need to search for the photo ID that doesn't match the individual wearing it."

"It might be hard to notice with all the people attending, but it's something else to consider. Also, this guy must be easy on the eye. Young girls will not speak to an old, ugly guy. He will be in great shape, possibly tan, nice hair, and clothes."

"You ladies are funny because Ivey said that very thing last night in our debrief meeting. I'll convey your agreement to Ivey. If she needs help to spot this guy, I'll have her ask for your help. Ivey is waving at me. Take care, Sheriff. See you soon." Bud ends the call even though I am not ready to let him go.

As I sit at my desk, I daydream about working for the FBI handling cases with Ivey and Bud. Their cases are much more complicated than anything I've dealt with until this murder spree. The FBI is involved in everything from serial rapists, murderers, arsonists to terrorists. The more I think about it, the more I think I'll stay here in my hometown. I'll let them worry about the hardcore crimes.

The overnight deputies report no sighting of the box truck as they enter the office to clock out. Also, the box truck at the warehouse sits in the same spot. I thank them and send them home for rest. At my wit's end, I place another call to the warehouse owner and add the word "urgent" in my message. I don't expect to receive a callback, but I am not ready to give up yet.

The rest of the morning, I concentrate on the budget. Things fall into place as I manage to find available money for an additional deputy. I've been working on additional staffing for over a year. We have stretched the sheriff's office to its max a few times over the past two years. Employees take a vacation, get sick, have babies, get married, and need time off. Well, now, things will be different around here. As soon as the council approves the budget, I will recruit an additional deputy. With more people moving into the area, adding personnel will happen more often than the council wants. Adding a new employee gives me something to think about. I pull out my employee handbook and place it on my desk. This is a subtle reminder to review it. If it needs updates, now will be an excellent time to make them.

My phone dings, so I glance at the screen, read the text from Bud, and my entire body tenses. Another girl is missing from the competition. The investigation into her disappearance has just begun. He advises he will call later and asks me to say a prayer.

My emotions run in circles. I feel bad for the FBI team and the parents of the missing girls. Without having children of my own, I can only imagine what they are going through. Not knowing the whereabouts of your child would be a horrible experience for any parent. The notion of helplessness could destroy a person.

"Hi, Sheriff," Taylor says while leaning on the doorframe of my office.

"Oh, hi, Taylor."

"Are you okay, Sheriff? You looked far away when I walked up."

"Bud sent me a text a few minutes ago. Another girl is missing from the cheerleading competition. She went missing this morning." I explain my demeanor.

"Another girl? I spoke with Ivey last night about Tori. They have no leads to follow. No witnesses came forward to help them either. That's just awful. I stopped by your office to find out if Bud has given you any idea about when they might be home. Ivey was uncertain, but with another girl missing, I don't expect them to come back soon."

"You're probably right, Taylor. I am

looking forward to them coming back, too. But I also want them to find the killer. We've been working on it for too long, and too many girls are dead because of this guy. Bud or Ivey will give us an update later. We'll wait on that."

Taylor turns and walks down the hallway toward the bullpen. This case frustrates us because the killer is so elusive. He's been doing it for a while now, and the stats show it's time for him to slip up and make a mistake. When he does, we'll be there.

A little while later, I walk to the bullpen, "Taylor, want to go to the diner for lunch?" He didn't bother with an answer. As he stands from his chair, he notifies dispatch of his location in case they might need him. While I wait for him to meet me at the door, Bud sends a message. They are working on the second missing girl's case. So, this morning within a few hours, two girls are missing from the cheerleading competition.

"Taylor, you will not believe this," I say as I put my phone back in my pocket.

"Yeah, I can guess. Ivey texted me that another girl is missing. So, that's two today, and that's crazy, Sheriff. This guy is bold. He takes girls from public places without causing a scene. I want to know what he promises these girls in return for them following him. Let's eat while we can."

We walk to the diner. The weather is hot and humid. I feel like a rain shower will grace us later today. Breathing the humid air is hard. By the time we enter the diner, I am soaked with sweat. "We should have driven. Now, I need a shower." I say as I wipe sweat from my forehead.

"You'll be fine, Sheriff. Your uniform will dry quickly in the air conditioning." Taylor says with a chuckle.

Lunch is excellent, as always. The diner is the best place to eat in the county. That's why people always pack it. We arrive before the crowd, which is nice for a change. We are paying our tabs when my cell phone rings. I point to the name on the screen and motion that I will be outside talking to Bud.

I listen to Bud as he describes a miserable day for them. Now three girls are missing. The second and third girls vanished just like Tori. They've been identified as Candice Jeffers and Phoebe Turner, both from South Carolina. They attend different high schools, but they are friends through cheerleading. The tournament coordinators canceled the rest of the competition because of the investigations. The team is packing up their gear. They are working with the police to notify the girls' families and question the attendees. Once this concludes, they will head back.

When Taylor walks up, I finish with Bud. I explain the situation in Florida to Taylor. He can't believe the number of missing girls. "How many more girls will this guy abduct before someone captures him?"

"I don't have a clue, Taylor. Bud and Ivey had hoped they would catch him while in Tallahassee. Our strategy sounded solid from all aspects, from video surveillance to the people on foot inside the arena. I guess there was no way to foresee the outcome of any strategy."

With nothing else to offer, we walk back to the office in silence. Our minds are tired, and our bodies tense. There have been no sightings of the box truck and no return call from the warehouse owner. Maggie meets us at the door, "Sheriff, a member of the press is in your office. They refused to leave. Tuttle is with him."

"Thanks, Maggie. Taylor, you're with me."

We walk in to meet an enormous man sitting in a chair across from my desk. It appears Tuttle and this man are having a staring contest. Apparently. Tuttle won. The man looks at me as we enter. "I'm Sheriff Steele. Can I help you?"

"Yes, ma'am. My name is Clyde Sutters from Mississippi. I'm following the murders of the girls, and I'm hoping to ask you some questions about the girls found in the ditch."

I glance at Tuttle and Taylor first before proceeding. "What questions do you want to ask, Mr. Sutters? Are you with the press?"

"Call me Clyde. Everybody does. I'm with the press, but we are a small-town newspaper. The first question I have pertains to shoes. Were the murdered girls found without shoes?"

"Yes. Now that I think about it, Clyde, I will refer you to the FBI since they are diligently working on this case to capture the guy responsible," I respond.

"Well, Sheriff, I hate that. No one from the FBI will speak to me. I get the same spiel with every call, and I am interested in the case because I am related to one of the first victims. I want to see this guy captured or, better yet, dead."

"May I suggest your quest ends here and now? You leave the case to the FBI. They will solve it one way or the other. If you have a business card, leave it, and one of my contacts will call you with an update."

"Here it is. Thanks for confirming the information regarding the shoes. It proves the murders are connected." Clyde reaches across the desk and lays his business card down.

The three of us stand back and watch Clyde leave the office. "Someone follow him and get his tag number, too. I want to know what he is doing. His card confirms he is with a newspaper, but I still want eyes on him."

Taylor answers, "I'm on him, Sheriff. I'll grab an unmarked car."

"Keep in contact, Taylor. Tuttle, did he discuss anything with you?"

"Nothing different from what he told you. He wasn't angry or anything, just stubborn. I didn't want to leave him alone in your office."

"Thanks for hanging with him." Tuttle exits the office as I ponder the intrusion. So, now we have a reporter from Mississippi following the case—literally. He traveled to Georgia to find the connection, and I confirmed it for him. Swell.

The afternoon meanders along with phone calls, a car accident report, and a jail inmate from a neighboring county being transported to our jail. The inmate had roomies that were not nice to him, so the sheriff requested he move to our jail. Our facilities can house inmates separately from the general population. With Captain Grayson handling the prisoner intake, I head home.

On the drive home, I remind myself to check my phone. I don't recall receiving any messages, but I don't want to miss Bud's update. If I am lucky, they should be on their way back from Florida. I'm ready to see Bud and Ivey, even though it's only been two days. They were busy in Florida and not the way they wanted. Three more missing girls from right under their noses. That had to sting, knowing they were right there and couldn't stop the killer from snatching more victims.

As I pull into my driveway, I notice pieces of mail scattered on the ground under the mailbox. I walk toward the mailbox, taking in my surroundings, and nothing seems unusual. Scooping up the mail on the ground and removing the piece still inside, I walk back to the house. Something doesn't feel right—is someone watching me? Or was someone verifying this house is mine by perusing my mail? I inspect my surrounding one last time before closing the door.

My plans for the night include a long, hot shower. Here's to hoping the shower will help lessen the pain from the knots in my upper body. The muscles in my shoulders and neck are full of tension and stress. Right now, I have too many knots to count.

By nine o'clock, I give up on Bud and Ivey coming back. I am curled up in the bed, reading a book, when my cell phone rings. Answering it on the second ring, I say, "Sheriff Steele."

"Sheriff, It's Bud. We had another incident this afternoon, so we haven't left yet. Tomorrow morning at the latest, we will head back."

"What happened now? Last I heard, you were helping with the witnesses. Any luck on that?"

"No luck with the witnesses. When we left the auditorium late in the afternoon, I spotted a box truck that fit our description. We tried to stop it, but it didn't want to stop, and a chase ensued. We lost the truck, but the police put out a BOLO, and one of their officers spotted it. A police officer engaged in another chase with the box truck. The driver of the truck entered the wrong way on the interstate and escaped yet again. Two chases later, we lost the truck. Can this trip get any worse? The trip has been a total bust from the get-go." Bud sighs.

"Oh, Bud. I am so sorry. However, if you think about it, you all were lucky the box truck driver didn't hit another vehicle and kill someone on the interstate. I don't blame the officers for not continuing the chase. That driver is gutsy! After the day you've had, you need not drive back tonight. Get some sleep. You will feel better in the morning."

"I'll talk with Ivey. She is pretty spent, too. Everyone on the team is a bundle of nerves. No one can believe the girls went missing from under our noses. It's hard to accept." Bud shares.

"Ok. You don't need to call me back. Just text me with your status. Be safe."

"Thanks, Jada."

As I end the call, my insides flutter. Every time he uses my name instead of Sheriff, I get that same sensation. I am falling for Bud, and he isn't even here. I'm glad he insisted on the talk before he left for Tallahassee. Now, to get him back to me, and let's see how long I get to keep him here. Sleep comes easily tonight, knowing Bud and Ivey will soon be back.

I awaken before the sun comes, startled by a text alert. Grabbing my phone from the nightstand, I read the message from Bud. They left Florida already. Quickly figuring drive time, I determine they will arrive mid-morning. There is no way I can go back to sleep, so I complete my morning routine and drive to the office.

Chapter 14

Once at the office, I walk around, gathering my daily updates. Our dispatchers have no news on the box truck. Captain Grayson processed the intake of the new prisoner. All is well there— no one has arrived in the bullpen, and Maggie's day hasn't started yet either. What was I thinking of coming in to work so early?

My office is cluttered again. I can't seem to keep ahead of the junk these days. By the time Bud and Ivey arrive, my office will be presentable, and all calls returned. I spend an hour with accounting on my budget again. I must prove my need for another deputy yet again. After this call, I should not have to discuss this again until next year. ATF hasn't returned my call on our marijuana plot. I will follow up with them later.

At ten o'clock, the two most missed people in the county walk into my office. It overjoys me with relief to see them. "You two look exhausted. Want to go take a nap before we catch up?"

Bud shares a glance with Ivey, and they shake their heads no. "I want to get caught up on the case and then spend time with you, and Ivey wants to see Taylor. Is he here?"

"Yes, I am, Bud. Am I late for the welcome home party?" Taylor asks from the doorway.

Ivey walks over to him and plants a kiss on his cheek, and we watch as Taylor reddens from the neck up. It is the cutest thing I have seen in a long time. Then Bud does the same to me, and everyone watches me turn red. It's cuter on someone else.

We add so much information to the board over the next two hours that we run out of space again. Everything points to the modeling offer and cheerleading. We are still without this guy's description.

"I almost forgot to tell you all. Taylor found a candy bar wrapper in the woods. We sent it to the crime lab, and they found a partial print. It's not enough to run through AFIS, but it will be enough for comparisons if we find prints."

As I sit across the table from Agent Ivey, the desire to question her about the possibility of us being related grows. I know this sounds crazy, but with the handwriting similarity and our backgrounds running along the path, I have a notion we are. I hope so, anyway. It would be nice for her to be a family member, mostly since Dad, my only family, is gone. The decision to ask her now or wait is grating on my nerves. I'm trying to concentrate, but it's difficult today.

With the updates discussed, we are at an impasse in the investigation. Bud and Ivey head into a conference call with the Tallahassee police. Taylor and I brainstorm new ideas about ways to capture this killer while the other two are away. Our thoughts turn out to be nothing new. We backtrack to the beginning of the case. Video and social media pop up as ideas. We've used both in the past few weeks, but we've just not found concrete evidence to help identify this guy. While we wait for the call to the end, my mind questions if I should tell Taylor about my suspicions of being related to Ivey. If I tell him, I'm not sure he would keep it a secret. He and Ivey are obviously close. That leaves Bud. Do I tell him? He is Ivey's partner, and I'm uncertain how close they truly are. I'm still keeping this secret to myself, hoping the right time will come for Ivey and me to discuss it.

I spend the rest of the day with Bud at the office. He continues working on the case using his contacts in Florida. We have dinner alone again. It gives us time to talk and continue the conversation we started before he left for Florida. He shares his thoughts of asking for a reassignment to Georgia so he will be closer to me. My heart explodes. I've had no one suggest they would make that kind of sacrifice for me. We walk to the car hand-in-hand. I drop him at the hotel wishing he would stay with me instead.

At home, I prepare for bed, realizing sleep will not come quickly. Bud and the future I can picture with him are on my mind. I've never had the luxury of dreaming about a man being in my life. I thought I was over trying to find one I could live with day in and day out with my career choice. I turn off my light and settle into bed when my phone rings. Ivey is the caller, and she wants to come over. She needs to talk about something, and she is ten minutes away.

"Hi, Ivey. I wasn't expecting anyone at this hour, so forgive the appearance. What's up?"

"Thanks for letting me come over so late, but I just left Taylor, and I didn't want the men to be here. I'm struggling because my relationship with Taylor is growing, and I don't know how to handle it. I like him and think we would make a great couple. But he is here, and I am in Louisiana, and that is too far for an actual relationship, I think. Taylor is your right hand, but do you think he would consider moving to Louisiana?"

"I am not the right person to ask, not because I don't want him to move, but because I can't stop him. He has a dream of being the next sheriff of this county. However, people's dreams change every day. Circumstances in life create changes. Have you considered moving to Georgia and getting reassigned? That might be an option for you."

"Not really. I don't want to lose Bud as a partner, and I would if I left Louisiana. We have been partners for a while now, and we work well together. The thought of learning a new one is daunting." Ivey looked down at her hands as she considered her options.

"Ivey, talk to Taylor and Bud. Tell them your thoughts. If you talk with them, their responses might shock you," I nudge, knowing Ivey's confession will elate Bud.

"You're right, Sheriff. I need to be on my way. Maybe I can get a decent night's sleep tonight. See you tomorrow." Ivey exits my house and walks toward her car.

"You too, Ivey. Be careful." I watch Ivey back out of the driveway and head towards town. Little does she know Bud is thinking the same thing.

I crawl back into bed with a picture forming in my mind. Would it be possible for Bud and Ivey to transfer to Georgia as partners? That would be incredible, although I'm not sure how the FBI handles personnel matters of this sort. Inevitably, agents move across the country for various reasons. The excitement builds with the possibility of Bud and Ivey working in Georgia. It would make Taylor happy, but I can't mention it to him. How can I keep this a secret?

Taylor and I arrive at the hotel at the same time the next morning, and we park side by side. We are joining Bud and Ivey for breakfast. We sit at our table in the back of the restaurant, drinking coffee. A few minutes later, Bud enters, and he looks around while he walks to the table. His expression is one of bewilderment. "Where's Ivey? She didn't answer the knock on her door."

"She hasn't made her appearance this morning. We arrived about ten minutes ago. Maybe she is still sleeping or in the shower. I'll walk up with you to check." Taylor suggests.

"We'll all go," I offer as Taylor and I get up from the table. I motion to the server and tell her our intention of returning to the table. She advises she will hold it.

The three of us enter the elevator, and our tense faces are visible in the door's reflection. Why didn't Ivey answer the knock? I didn't tell the men she was at my house late last night because the first question they will ask is, "Why was she there?" Then I must be the one to explain it, and she should be the one to tell Taylor her feelings.

Her door remains locked, and she doesn't answer after repeated attempts. "I'll go get the manager. He'll let us in."

The men stand staring at her door, willing it to open as I turn the corner for Ivey's room. The manager accompanies me and allows us in. I enter first, hoping to find her in the shower or getting dressed. Unfortunately, that doesn't happen. Her bed is made as if she never slept in it. If she didn't come back to the hotel last night, where did she go? My pulse races. All kinds of scary thoughts go through my mind.

"Guys, she's not here. It appears she didn't sleep in this bed last night. I must confess to you two. She was at my house last night at around midnight. We discussed personal stuff, and then she left shortly afterward. I watched her back out of the driveway. She said nothing about not going to the hotel. I just assumed this is where she would go."

Taylor studies his phone screen. "She's not answering her phone either. My calls go straight to voicemail. It's like her phone is turned off." His face shows me how upset he is, and there is nothing I can do to ease the pain.

Bud touches my arm. "Let's trace her drive from your house to the hotel. If Ivey was too tired to drive, she might have had an accident, and no one has found her yet."

We jog out of the hotel and jump into Taylor's car. Lights and sirens on, we race toward my house. I can't believe I didn't tell her to text me when she made it to the hotel. I was so excited to hear she wants a relationship with Taylor that I wasn't thinking about safety. With Ivey on my mind, I call dispatch and ask for a patrol car to search, too. If her car had been on the side of the road, I would have noticed it as I drove into town. So, why didn't I see it?

"How many roads take you into town from your house? I'm trying to figure out how many roads we need to search," Bud asks, not knowing his way around yet.

"There are two direct routes on main roads. Earlier, I stopped by the dry cleaners, so let's try the other way since I didn't see her on my way into town."

Taylor makes a turn and slows down so we can look on both sides as we drive along. A dark-colored car blends into woods and ditches. I get frustrated as we inch our way down the road. "Calm down, Sheriff. You are panting. You're getting worked up." Bud says from the backseat as he rubs my arm, obviously realizing how upset I am.

"I'm trying, Bud, but this is wild. With murdered girls in a ditch and now a missing FBI agent? It's too much." I take a deep breath hoping to calm myself.

"I promise you we will find her because I'm not giving her up," Taylor states emphatically. Since I can't bring myself to say anything, I keep my mouth shut. He has no idea what she was doing at my house last night. Do I tell him now or wait? If I wait and something happens to Ivey, I will never forgive myself. But if I tell him now, it will upset him, and I need him with a rational mind—or at least as rational as it can be under the circumstances.

We make two passes along the road from my house to the main road. There is no sign of a vehicle on either side of the road. "Taylor, drive back to my house and then start from there. We will travel in the same direction as she would have at the time, she went missing." I check in with dispatch as we start over. Her vehicle is nowhere near the hotel. A deputy is on the way to the Snappy Mart, just to make sure we cover all bases. After the Snappy Mart, I am at a loss as to her whereabouts.

Bud and Taylor hear the update from dispatch, so I don't repeat it. I plaster my eyes to the side window because there must be a sign of her. She was in a car, for God's sake. The car did not disappear. I glance back at Bud, and his face tells the story. He is distraught. The look of anguish is too much. Tears fill my eyes as I struggle to see past them. I don't have many close friends and Ivey was becoming one. The will to scream, throw, or shoot something is unbearable. Every imaginable emotion is wreaking havoc through my body. Blinking away the tears is useless.

"Sheriff, we'll find her. Don't cry. There are tissues in the glove box." Taylor offers.

"The tears won't stop. Too many emotions pent up, I guess. Where could she be? I am scared to death that the killer is back. Horrible things are running through my imagination." Bud reaches across the seat and places his hand on my arm. My body trembles with fear and adrenaline.

"Ivey is tough both physically and mentally. If she is in a terrible predicament, I have faith in her abilities to overcome it. Ivey is smart and stubborn, just like you. Think good thoughts, Sheriff." Bud's neck cranes to the left, searching that side of the road while he rubs my arm.

After the statement Bud makes about

Ivey, I swallow hard. The realization hits me. I haven't told Bud about my idea of Ivey being related to me. Wonder what he will say? Obviously, he sees the resemblance in the way we act—another hard conversation for me.

Bud sucks in a breath and states, "Stop the car. There it is Taylor. Slow down and pull off the road when you find a spot." Bud points to the car's location.

"Where is it, Bud? I don't see it. Are you sure you saw it?" I'm eager to see the car but tears blur my vision.

Taylor pulls over a little way up the road, and we exit the vehicle and run back to the spot Bud saw the car. "There," he points again, "see the black sedan tucked into the woods. I glimpsed a reflection."

We jump into the ditch and run over to the car. Taylor and I pull our service weapons before reaching the vehicle. We start our approach from the rear, and we slither up both sides to the front doors. The car is empty. Somehow, I expected that. Bud pops the trunk, and it is empty as well, except for a shotgun in a holster under the trunk lid. "That's interesting. There is no way someone could place Ivey in the trunk, and the weapon remains in place. The weapon would be the first thing Ivey grabbed, so whoever has her took her from the driver's seat."

Taylor calls out, "There is body damage to the car's right rear. Another vehicle might have forced Ivey off the road. That explains the damage, but who caused it."

We scour the area looking for clues she might be on foot. "Johnson and Rufus need to be here ASAP," I state more to myself than anyone.

While waiting for Johnson, we search for telltale signs that someone would leave if they were running from someone, like broken twigs, folded limbs, or blood. There wasn't anything useful found.

I share with the guys. "Johnson is here. I'll go back to meet him. Keep looking."

It takes a minute to bring Johnson up to date on Ivey. Johnson is just as shocked as the rest of us. "Sheriff, do you think someone deliberately forced her off the road last night? Why would they do that?"

"Johnson, I think it is intentional, and I believe it is our killer. The FBI team in Florida was close to him. The killer could recognize them, and he is desperate to keep his pleasures coming."

"Let's go, Rufus." Johnson looks around, "He needs something with Ivey's smell on it. What can we use?"

I hadn't thought of that. "Let's see if there is anything in the car."

All of us march back into the woods. I am beginning not to like these woods. Too many bad things are happening here. Once we make it to the car, I find a hair tie in the console, but that is it. "Will this work, Johnson? This is all I found of Ivey's."

"That should do it, Sheriff." Johnson takes it from me and gives Rufus his instructions.

Rufus puts his nose to the ground, lifts it in the air, puts it back to the ground, glances at Johnson, tugs on the leash, and they are off. I jog behind Johnson and Bud, and Taylor picks us up and joins in the search after redialing Ivey's phone. Rufus runs a hundred yards, turns around, runs back to the car, and then races down the side of the road. Rufus halts and alerts onto an object. Johnson reaches it first, and his face tells me all I needed to know. I feel like throwing up when I see the shoe in his gloved hand.

Taylor screams obscenities when he realizes it is Ivey's shoe. Bud's face pales. We look like death standing on the side of the road. Johnson is the only level-headed person on the road. "Guys over here. Another vehicle was parked here. Drag marks are here and here. However, there is no proof these drag marks are from Ivey. There is a spot here on the side of the shoe. I noticed it when I placed it in the evidence bag. The spot could be a partial fingerprint."

Bud finishes the picture for us. "Ivey left your house and headed back to the hotel. Someone tagged the back end of her car, she spun, ended up in the woods, the unknown vehicle stopped here and took her somewhere. Does that sound about right?"

"Dispatch, this is Sheriff Steele. Call the local hospital—see if someone matching Ivey's description was admitted overnight. This request is urgent. If you can't do it, find someone who can. I am waiting," I bark orders at the dispatcher.

The time it takes dispatch to call the hospital is grueling, even though I had the answer within minutes. We need to clear all avenues before true panic takes over. I receive the call on my cell phone. The dispatcher confirms my fear. No one matching Ivey's description has been admitted to the hospital, and I don't feel like the driver would transport an injured person across the county line.

"Ivey is not at the hospital, and that leaves two scenarios. She either walked away from the accident, and she hasn't checked in yet, or the killer kidnapped her. We will have her car moved to the impound lot. Johnson, take Taylor to the office and drop that shoe off ASAP! Once the car is in route to the office, I'll follow it back to the office."

The two deputies walk off toward Johnson's car—two men on a mission. Their shoulders are back, and they hold their heads high. With these men on my team, how can we lose this fight? The panic subsides in my bones, and I know we will find Ivey, but where? The woods where we found Tonya and the area behind the Snappy Mart need searching again. Other than those two locations, I'm not sure where to go from there.

Bud waits with me for the tow truck. We lean on the patrol car and stare out into space. Bud asks questions that I can't answer. "Did the killer follow us back here from Florida? How long has he been tailing us? How did he find your house?"

"I hadn't thought about the last question. The first two questions I can't answer. If the killer followed Ivey, then yes, he knows where I live. Don't ask me to leave because I'm not running away. If anything, I hope he comes by for a visit. I'll be ready for him."

"Oh, no, you don't. There is no way you are staying there alone. I'll be there, or if you don't want me to stay with you, Taylor can," Bud states.

The tow truck pulls up, giving me a pass on responding. Ivey's car is ready to be loaded onto the flatbed as soon as the truck driver hooks it up. The car makes a screeching noise as they drag it through the woods and up the side of the ditch. It may never be roadworthy again after that ordeal. We follow the truck to the lot and then go inside to find Taylor.

Taylor, Tuttle, and Johnson sit hunched over their computers when we walk into the bullpen. They are scouring surveillance videos from town. "Find anything useful yet?"

Tuttle answers, "Not conclusive, but we

found a box truck driving through town. The driver passes the bank, and the ATM camera caught a small portion of the truck's side. Taylor is trying to track him by finding him on another camera."

"Taylor, what's your status? Do you have anything yet?"

"Nothing, Sheriff. He turned off the main street. The next camera would be the CVS by the pharmacy drive-through. The truck doesn't show on their feed."

"Ok. So that means he turned to the left, across the street from the CVS, then back right again, which would avoid all cameras in the immediate area. Someone planned Ivey's accident, or he got lucky when she came to my house alone, and he acted on impulse."

Bud counters, "If he acted on impulse, did he have a place to take her here, or is she in Tallahassee? The killer's home base remains a mystery, and he could conceivably be anywhere."

"Don't think like that. Ivey must be nearby. As a general rule, kidnappers don't transport victims too far if they try to escape or meet outside sources. That would draw attention to him, and he is aware we are looking for him," I counter.

Bud nods as if he agrees. We are all on edge, but we push through the rest of the day. By supper, we are starving since we missed breakfast and lunch. While we are eating, Bud tells the table he is staying at my house. Bud explains his reason by blaming the kidnapper as there is the possibility the kidnapper saw my house.

"You need not explain a thing, Bud. We agree someone needs to stay with you, Sheriff. Everyone needs to stay alert, just in case. The killer is aware we are on his tail, and he may try to finish us all at some point. If you feel you want more than Bud, we can take turns staying on the couch."

"Thanks, guys, but I think Bud is sufficient. I can't think of anything else to do tonight, so let's finish supper, and then we will start fresh in the morning. Dispatch will continue the roving patrols around the warehouse as a precaution. There is something sketchy with that owner." It makes me wonder why a businessman isn't returning phone calls from a sheriff.

The group eats in silence as thoughts race through our heads, trying to piece this puzzle together. "I forgot to tell you this morning—ATF is taking the marijuana plot, at least for now." This relieves Taylor and Tuttle. They didn't want that worry.

"That's one thing you can take off of your plate," Bud states.

Taylor estimates the number of plants, and Bud is all ears. After the story, Bud agrees the plot is probably local. If it were for a large-scale distribution outfit, the number of plants would be ten times the number you found. Bud thinks someone here is growing it for their personal use, but he may also sell a small portion. I am glad ATF took the lead on this one.

Once supper is over, we part ways. Bud and I stop by the hotel, grab his gear, and go to my house. The guy's head off in other directions. Taylor is driving by the warehouse, but I advised him not to engage in anything without backup.

Everything is in order at my home upon our arrival. The doors remain locked, and it appears no one has tampered with them. We settle in for the night. However, it seems weird enjoying Bud at home when Ivey is missing and possibly injured or worse. She might be dead. Sitting on the sofa, we work through the case again, trying to piece together the missing parts. I am terrified for Ivey and mad at the person who took her. Above all else, I need confirmation she is my sister.

Chapter 15

"Bud, I want to share something with you, but I don't want you to think I'm crazy. So, listen to me before you throw questions at me. Okay?"

"This sounds like you're going to tell me you don't want me around."

"Heavens no. Not even close to that. Something has been on my mind for a few weeks, and I haven't had the nerve to mention it to anyone. But with Ivey missing, I need to tell someone I trust, and you fall in that category."

"I'm all ears. Talk." Bud leans back on the sofa with one arm across the back. His action proves to me he is open to my commentary.

"I'm not sure how to phrase it, so I am just going to spill it. I think Ivey and I are sisters or are at least related in some way." With my hand raised to stop the questions, I continue. "Think about it. I grew up with just a dad, and she grew up with just a mom. Both of our feature's favor in some ways. We walk alike, we're both interested in police work and sports, and last but not least, the handwriting matches."

"Stop there. What handwriting matches?" Intrigued, Bud leans forward, concentrating on my revelation.

I walk over to the bookcase, remove the

photo of dad and me, and show Bud the handwriting from the card's back. He studies it for a few seconds then asks for the comparison. I had taken a picture of Ivey's writing on the murder board from a few days ago. When I produce the photo of the board, Bud takes both samples and compares them.

"Jada, I am amazed you put this together by yourself. The handwriting is too distinct not to be a match. What brought all this on? What was the trigger that set it in motion?"

"When Ivey talks, thoughts jump into my mind that I've met her before. Then we look at each other and sometimes, we say the same thing at the same time. Once I saw Ivey's handwriting, it confirmed my suspicions. My guess is our parents split when Mom was pregnant with Ivey. I don't think Dad ever knew she was pregnant. If he had, he would have provided for Ivey. Dad was the kind of man who protected what was his. He always told me Mom wanted to go back home to her parents, and she didn't want to live in Georgia with a baby and a sheriff for a husband. Mom had a healthy fear of what could happen to a police officer."

"What are the odds you two would run into each other here, in your county? I can't believe you have been working on this in the background while holding down your job plus working on this case. You are amazing, and I love you for it." Bud states.

"My idea may be total craziness, but I want your opinion before I mention it to Ivey. Now that she is missing, I want the truth. Also, I need to confess why Ivey came to my house last night. After her time with Taylor, Ivey wanted to discuss her options. She adores Taylor, and she doesn't want to see their relationship end. Ivey wants to speak with you about the possibility of her transferring to Georgia so she and Taylor could work on their relationship." The transformation on Bud's face turns to pure happiness. Bud smiles that fabulous smile that makes me melt.

"Are you serious? So, Ivey and Taylor are in the same situation? From sisters to partners in a relationship. This gets better and better. The big question is—does Taylor know why she was at your place last night?" Bud questions.

I shake my head from side to side as I state, "No, and he hasn't asked, and I really don't want to tell him. I'd rather Ivey tell him how she feels and what she is thinking. It need not come from me unless she doesn't come back. At that point, I would want him to know how she felt about him."

"That I can understand. If you were in Ivey's position, I would want to know how you felt about me. That would give me some peace to deal with the aftermath. There is a lot to work out between us. The thought of you being sisters shocks me. Now that I think about it, I recall several instances where you sounded alike or did something that surprised me. You and Ivey are similar in your characteristics. It wouldn't surprise me at all if you are sisters."

"From my heart, I would be ecstatic. Since Dad passed, I don't have a family here. There are a few cousins scattered around the country, but no one I am close with. I would be grateful for a sister. Then, with you around, my world would be complete." I express my sentiment the best I can. Sharing my personal feelings is not something I often do.

"What are you saying, Jada? Tell me." Bud's eyes plead with me to say it out loud.

"I love you, Bud, and I want you to stay with me now and in the future. I'm not sure how we will work around our careers, but together we can accomplish anything."

Bud jumps up from the sofa, picks me up, and then swings me around the living room. "I've been waiting for that. If I could have read your mind, I wouldn't have been so anxious about it. But, thankfully, you've come to your senses! I love you, Jada."

"It sounds good to say it. I shouldn't have waited this long, but relationships are hard for me. Thank you for being patient."

"Why don't you check in with the office, and then we need sleep. Tomorrow will be busy in our quest to find Ivey." Bud suggests.

I do as he requests. Dispatch has had no reports of any kind since we left the office. That could be good or bad, depending on how you thought about it. We are both sound asleep as soon as we lay down. Nerves and adrenaline in one day will physically exhaust a person.

The next day starts cloudy and gloomy. Dark clouds pass overhead, just waiting to release the rain. Bud and I drive by the location where we found Ivey's vehicle. When I see it again, my heart clenches. Bud holds my hand because he knows what I am thinking. We might never see her again.

People are active at the sheriff's office when we arrive. The press left a message for me to call. How did the media find out about Ivey already? Today is visitation day at the jail. That always makes for exciting days. Some days are calm while other visitation days turn violent. The sheriff's department has endured fist fights and knife fights in the parking lot. Luckily no serious injuries.

Bud calls his boss and discusses the situation with Ivey while I call the press and stall them as much as possible. The press didn't acknowledge Ivey's status. Once the call ends, we meet in the bullpen. Taylor and Johnson wait on us while Tuttle is already out on patrol. Taylor, with dark circles under his eyes, tries to smile at us, but you can tell he is hurting. I doubt he slept at all last night.

"Hey, guys. Any recent developments on Ivey? Bud called his office and updated them. If the kidnapper is after money, we would have expected a ransom demand by now. So, we will spend today searching for Ivey."

"No developments, Sheriff. I drove around all night looking in different areas of the county because I couldn't sit still, and I couldn't sleep, so I drove. There were people in and out of the Snappy Mart most of the night. No box trucks. It makes me wonder if the killer just happened upon Ivey alone in her car."

"There's no guarantee the killer won't try something with us as well. Everyone needs to stay alert until we capture this guy. I am hoping the results from the fingerprint from Ivey's shoe will come through."

Johnson adds, "The crime lab advises it will be lunchtime before they have something. The print is more like a smear, and they are working to clean it up. If they can, it will only be partial, but it will be enough to run through AFIS. If he is in the system, we will get him."

"Lunchtime? The techs can't get it done before then?" Stomping off to my office, I mutter that a fingerprint should not take hours to recover and run through the system. I call the crime lab, expressing my concern about the delay. Once I explain the inquiry's seriousness, the lab tech says I will have it within the hour. I hang up, telling him the clock is ticking.

I sit at my desk for a minute to calm my nerves. Between a headache and my rising blood pressure, I am not feeling so good. The guys in the bullpen wait on me for an update from the crime lab, so I give them one, "The crime lab will provide the results of the print within the hour." I spout.

"Way to go, Sheriff. There is no plausible reason they can't have done it sooner." Johnson adds. He stands and looks at me, "I'm going on patrol. Call if you need me."

Taylor jumps up and says "Ditto" and follows Johnson.

They walk out to the parking lot under a cloudy sky. Words do not seem appropriate for what Taylor, and the rest of us, are going through. I've never endured a missing officer before, and I can say I don't like it. In my law enforcement studies, I have never run across the type of person who would kidnap a law enforcement officer. Some words come to mind: deranged, desperate, crazy. If I take the time, I'm sure more would come to mind.

Bud enters my office with a grin on his face. "A witness came forward in Tallahassee who claims they saw a man holding a girl by her upper arm. The man and girl appeared to be talking. Neither one seemed angry, and the girl was actually smiling. The witness didn't come forward at the time because it looked normal until she saw the girl's picture on the TV. One of our artists is meeting the witness today so that they can provide a sketch. The picture will be available midafternoon."

"Finally! We need this. The print should be ready in an hour and then the description sometime today. We are getting somewhere! Do you think this killer took Ivey back to Florida or back to where it all started?" I question while staring at the murder board.

"Ivey is here. The killer took her as a warning to us to back off. He has no intention of getting caught. The killer thinks he is too good to get caught, but we can guarantee his capture. On the flip side, if he is as desperate as we think, he might try to take another one of us."

"Every employee at the Sheriff's office received notice to stay vigilant and travel in pairs if possible. I don't think I can handle another missing person."

Maggie's voice comes over the speaker requesting my presence. Something in her voice makes me jog to her desk. "Sheriff Tuttle radioed in he has a box truck that fits the BOLO description, and he is in pursuit on Route 33."

"Ok. Maggie. I'm on it."

Bud follows me to Maggie's desk. "I'm riding shotgun, Sheriff," Bud says with a twinkle in his eye.

We sprint to the car. I grab the mic from its holder. "Tuttle, Sheriff Steele. What's your location?" Pausing for a reply, I'm surprised that none comes. I repeat myself as my pulse rate increases. Just as I click the mic, Tuttle replies.

"Sheriff, Tuttle. The truck is swerving on the roadway. The driver refuses to let me pass. He spun around and are headed back towards the Snappy Mart. Is there anyone else on patrol?"

"10-4. Taylor, did you receive a call? Lights and sirens. Stop the driver with a pit maneuver."

"10-4." Taylor replies as sirens blare through the radio.

Tires squeal as we exit the parking lot. My heart sits in my throat as this is our chance to bring the killer in and find Ivey. A thought hits me, and I grab the mic again. "Sheriff to all responding deputies—we need him alive. He is the only one who knows where he is holding Agent Ivey."

All respond with a "10-4," even though I'm sure some must question my request. Taylor wants to see this man in the ground, and I can't blame him. However, Ivey comes first. We have to find her, and then we can take care of the killer.

I press the pedal down as far as I dare. Dust is visible in the air from a half-mile away. Two deputies and I are in a chase with potentially catastrophic ramifications. Bud looks over at me as he grips the dashboard and asks, "Do you think Ivey is in the back of the truck? Is that why he is running like this?"

"I hope not, Bud. This guy is beyond reckless. The truck slides across the road onto the shoulder, and then somehow, he recovers it. Let's pray she isn't in there because if she is conscious, it is the scariest ride she has ever had."

The cars follow the truck as it zigzags across the county. Mile after mile, we watch and wonder in amazement. Taylor gets a jump on the truck at a four-way stop aiming for the left rear quarter panel. The driver sees what Taylor is about to do and turns the truck back into our path while taking evasive action to avoid contact. So now, we head in the opposite direction. Soon, the truck turns onto an unmarked road and continues at a high rate of speed. At least the deputies are familiar with this road as it leads to a dead-end where the driver will need to make a right or left or end up in a pond.

I prepare for the truck entering the pond as I slow my approach. The county doesn't need three of its patrol cars in a crash. The truck slides into a turn at the end of the road and somehow keeps it on all four wheels. "I don't think the driver slowed down at all to make that turn. Someone must make him stop, or he will continue until his truck is out of gas or he kills another person." Bud stated as he watched in amazement.

"You're right. This guy refuses to stop. We need to do a pit maneuver now, but I don't want him injured. We need him alive and talking. The driver is the only person who might know where Ivey is being held." I grimace as I watch Taylor slide off the road. It doesn't take him long to recover, but it allows Tuttle room to pass him. Now, Tuttle is in the lead and directly behind the truck.

"Dispatch, notify surrounding counties of our pursuit. The sheriff's department is not relinquishing pursuit. This guy is ours." I state sternly as Bud looks at me, "What? Why are you staring at me?"

"You are a good multi-tasker. Here you are driving in a car chase, one-handed while talking on the radio and giving orders, and you never once slowed down to do it all. You are amazing, Jada." Bud's face showed me he meant every word he said to me.

"Thanks, but it really is part of the job." My eyes move back to the road in time to see Tuttle try a pit maneuver. He doesn't hit the truck in the right place because it jogs to the right, and then the driver recovers and continues. "Do you think there is a product in the back of the truck? With the attempted maneuver, I expected the truck to spin. It shouldn't be that heavy as long as the back is empty."

"The truck might be full, but if it is, the weight should shift and help us turn it over or at least cause it to slide off the road," Bud answers as Tuttle comes over the radio.

"Sheriff, Tuttle. The driver is holding a handgun out the window. He is pointing the gun downward. No shots yet, so I guess he just wants us to see it."

"10-4 Tuttle. Stop him when you get a

chance but prepare for anything when we approach the subject. This takedown won't be easy."

"10-4 Sheriff," Tuttle replies.

The truck runs from us at high speed while the tires spew gravel and dirt. Our cars sustain pot marks on the grills and hood along with the windshield. When the stone strikes the vehicle, the noise sounds as if we are in a hailstorm. The truck driver swerves from side to side on the roadway. He is expecting us to attempt to stop him somehow. The three patrol cars continue the chase, unsure of what the next curve will bring.

As the truck makes another unusual move, he turns into the path of an ambulance. The ambulance swerves and clips Tuttle's vehicle as he passes it. Neither Tuttle nor the rest of us stop for the accident. Bud and I listen as Tuttle calls dispatch to advise them of the crash with the ambulance. Tuttle will complete the report after he stops this killer.

"That accident could have been a bad one. I'm glad they were not running sirens." I state after Tuttle ends his conversation with dispatch. How much further can he drive? We've traveled miles, and this guy doesn't appear to be stopping. So, it's time we stop him.

"Tuttle, Taylor, if you see a way to stop the driver, do it."

Both guys respond with a "10-4." I suck in my breath, waiting for my deputies to stop this chase. It's coming, but how long will they wait? Here we go down yet another road. This road allows for more room for the truck to swerve.

We continue following Taylor as he follows Tuttle, who remains in close contact with the truck. When the truck driver swerves, Taylor backs off Tuttle's vehicle. Tuttle is so close to the back of the truck that if something happens, we could all be in danger.

The anticipation ramps up and sweat runs down my back. As I hold the steering wheel with one hand, I wipe the sweat from my brow. The truck hits a pothole and leans to the right. As it does this, Tuttle hits the left rear quarter panel and sends the truck careening into the ditch. The driver knows he can't keep the truck out of the ditch, so he jumps out of the door before the truck stops and runs away from the scene.

We slam the cars into park, jump out, and continue the chase on foot. The driver enters the woods while shouting at us. He tells us what he will do to Ivey. Taylor and Tuttle are closest to him, and they yell back. The driver fires a shot toward our location. All four of us hit the ground as the bullet sails through the woods over our heads. The foot chase continues, and this time we gain on him. The driver trips over a log and reaches down at his ankle as he tries to escape. He props himself up on his elbow, and he glances at our distance.

I call out to the driver by stating my name and why we want to speak with him. All I get for my troubles is another gunshot aimed at me. It doesn't matter who I am or why we want him. His goal is to escape. After ducking another bullet, I take up the chase again.

Another fifty yards brings another bullet toward my group. The bullet slices Tuttle's upper left arm, and he and Taylor shoot back. Two bullet wounds appear on the runner's chest, and he falls to the ground, bleeding profusely. I call dispatch and give our location for extraction.

"Here, place this on his wounds and apply pressure." Bud produces two packs of gauze and advises us on how to control the blood loss stemming from the bullet wounds. "We've got to keep him alive." Bud continues to monitor the blood loss.

The desperation in Bud's voice is real, as is his concern for Ivey. Just like the rest of us, but probably even more so. Bud and Ivey have been together for years. Bud is Ivey's only partner.

Tuttle's arm is blood-drenched to the point that drops fall from his fingers. "Tuttle, your arm. Do we have any gauze left? We need to stop your bleeding." I ask the group with my eyes on Bud.

No one produces gauze since we gave it to the perpetrator. "My belt will work as a tourniquet to help slow the bleeding." Bud rips his belt from the loops and wraps it around Tuttle's arm. "Here we go, Tuttle. This will hurt."

Tuttle flinches as Bud tightens the belt around his arm. The belt doesn't stop the flow completely, but it slows it. Tuttle props himself up next to a tree while we work on the driver. The driver turns a grayish color as Bud and Taylor press the gauze to his chest. Taylor tries to get the driver to speak, but it's apparent he is unconscious.

The same ambulance Tuttle struck during our chase arrives at our rescue. They understand now what was happening and jump in to save the driver. Ten minutes later, we are carting the driver out while Bud helps Tuttle walk to the ambulance. Tuttle is pale but otherwise in good spirits. He makes a trip to the same hospital.

Once we help load the driver and Tuttle into the ambulance, we open the back of the truck. It's empty. I'm unsure how I was supposed to feel seeing it empty. We searched the truck and found a gun on the floorboard under the driver's seat. I guess that is the driver's hiding place for it. Bud and I grin when we check the magazine. A 9mm bullet falls from the magazine into Bud's hand. We bag the gun and bullet into evidence.

I notified dispatch to handle the truck removal from the ditch, and Bud asks them to run the plates to determine the owner. Then, I

213

acknowledge we will be at the hospital with Tuttle and the driver.

Our arrival at the emergency room is quite the scene. Two patrol cars with sirens follow an ambulance into the hospital entrance. The ambulance attendants have a surgeon waiting at the door, so they whisk the driver away before we have the chance to get his name. A nurse escorts Tuttle into an exam room while the rest of us find chairs in the waiting room.

Chapter 16

Time stands still. I can't believe both of my deputies shot this guy. It shouldn't shock me, but I was hoping we would take him alive and talking, not alive and barely breathing. How can I look at Bud and feel good about the situation? Ivey's location remains unknown. Bud is probably raging mad at the deputies for shooting him, and I can't blame him—nor could I blame my guys. There is nothing like being stuck in the middle.

Maggie calls with the stolen truck report. The truck's owner is from Lamar County, Mississippi, and his name is Stuart Milton Boards. I don't have a response. The Lamar County Sheriff is the one who gave me fits. That will be an interesting phone call later.

As we wait for word on Tuttle and the driver, a nurse stops by our room to deliver an update. "Deputy Tuttle is doing okay. The bullet sliced through the top layer of muscle. No damage, but that area bleeds a lot. He is getting stitched up as we speak. The doctor will release him shortly. However, the driver is in grave condition. The surgery is going well as it can. He lost a tremendous amount of blood. It will be a while before he is stable. Get comfortable if you plan on staying."

Bud speaks up, "We need this guy alive.

He is holding one of our agent's hostage, and we do not know the location. If he wakes up, we need to speak to him immediately."

The nurse replies, "I will share your situation with the staff." We watch as the nurse turns and exits the room.

"That doesn't sound too promising, now does it?" Bud asks as he looks at Taylor and me.

Both of us answer with a resounding "No." Taylor leans over with his elbows on his knees, knowing he helped put the driver in the hospital.

We sit in silence, wondering if this guy will make it or not. If he doesn't, what do we do next? With hospital staff in and out of the surgical area, I never realized how busy the hospital is until now. Back when Dad was Sheriff, I can remember the hospital being one floor with two wings. Now, it takes up a city block and then some. They've even brought in some doctors from other more prestigious hospitals in the state to work here. The patient population has undoubtedly grown.

Tuttle rounds the corner and sees us sitting in the waiting room. "Any news on the driver?"

I stand and hug him. "A better question is, how is your arm? And no news on the driver."

He explains, "The bullet grazed my upper left arm. There is no damage except for the blood loss. The doctor stitched me up and sent me here. I am also cleared for duty as long as I cover the stitches, and you agree, of course."

"Unfortunately, with the shooting, the GBI will investigate the circumstances for both you and Taylor. Both of you will be on paid leave until we conclude the investigation. It shouldn't take long. I've already called them to meet me here."

"Somehow, that doesn't seem fair. We shot a potential killer who was firing at us, to begin with." Tuttle spouts while trying to explain his position.

"I understand, Tuttle. But the law is the law, right? Once they find out who's in custody, they might relinquish the investigation until after we find Ivey. I will ask and see if they will agree. Why don't you let Taylor take you home so you can rest? We will call with any change in the driver's condition."

"I'm not going anywhere. I'll stretch out and rest in the chairs over in the corner because I don't want to miss anything." Tuttle stands and walks to the corner and looks around.

This time, Bud stands, "I'll push the chairs together. You need to prop your arm on something. It will help with the pain once the numbing medication wears off."

"Well, Bud. You sound like you experienced a similar type of wound. Care to share?" Tuttle asks.

"It was a long time ago, but yes, a bullet

grazed me in about the same place you were. It leaves a nice scar you can show off to your lady friends," Bud offers.

Taylor joins the conversation, "Did you get the guy that shot you, Bud?"

"Sure, we did. He is in prison on death row. He shot and killed two police officers that day. I testified against him and was proud to do it, although I spent several years in therapy. Have you ever heard of survivor's guilt? I had it bad, and the FBI made me go through the therapy. Good thing I didn't fight it. I needed it."

I look over at Bud. He told the guys something very personal, something I didn't know. Jealousy is not an emotion I am used to, but I can say I am a little jealous that the guys heard the story before I did. It relaxes Bud to be around my group of deputies. Wonder if he would consider working for the sheriff's office instead of the FBI? Having someone with his experience on the team would be great.

The rest of the day is slow. The nurses stop in every so often and share that the driver remains unconscious after surgery. His condition is grave. They removed two bullets from him, and the doctor has them for the GBI. They will update us when his status changes.

Deputy Johnson stops by the hospital to check on us and take the evidence bag to the lab. We want Doc James to compare the gun we found in the truck against the girl's wounds. My guess is someone shot the girls using the gun we have in evidence. Now, I need Doc James to back up that thought with a scientific test.

I can't talk Taylor, Bud, or Tuttle into leaving the hospital and getting rest. They want me to go, but I refuse. There is no way I am leaving the hospital. I want to be here when this guy wakes up. The more time that lapses, the more nervous I get. How long can Ivey hang on, and where is she? Is she hurt? If so, how bad?

Since everyone stays, we settle in for the night. As we sit in the waiting room, we discuss strategies for handling if the driver dies or survives. If he dies, we must find his hideaway—somewhere he can keep a person from being discovered. If he survives, we must get him to give up his hiding place. The doctors agree to allow us time to question him once he is lucid enough to understand our questions. We ask the doctors to please ask the driver where he is holding Ivey, especially if they think he is dying. The midnight update is promising in his recovery.

The smell of coffee wakes me up. As I pry my eyes open, I stare at Bud. I could get used to that smile. "Good morning, Sheriff. Coffee and donuts for everyone."

"Where is everyone?" I ask, concerned.

"Taylor and Tuttle stepped out to the men's room. Tuttle is a little unsteady, but with food, he should bounce back. A nurse is meeting him here so she can change the bandage on his arm. I think she likes him. Watch her smile at him."

"Any word on the driver? I would like to know his name, too. Wonder if they found any identification on him?" Questions keep flowing as my head clears.

"We haven't received an update this morning. But we should soon. Shift change has just taken place. Here come Taylor and Tuttle now."

Along with Taylor and Tuttle, an older man follows them into the room. I stand waiting for him to approach me. Instead, he sticks his hand out to Bud. He introduces himself as the GBI investigator. I watch Bud, and after a pause, I stick my hand out and introduce myself. GBI investigator Sullens stammers when he realizes I'm the Sheriff.

Sullens apologizes for his error, and we step off to the side and discuss the situation. I give Sullens a rundown of the events leading to the shooting. He needs statements from Taylor and Tuttle to satisfy his requirements. He experienced a similar episode with a partner years ago. His eyes turned sympathetic when I told him of Ivey's predicament. I promised him those statements, and Sullens hands me a business card with instructions to have our reports emailed to him. He reminded me time is of the essence. Sullens agreed to leave Taylor and Tuttle on the force until he reviewed the statements. He realizes his actions are a little out of the box. But he's been in their shoes. Once he receives them, then he would make his decision. We shook hands, and I ushered him out the door.

When I faced the guys, their eyes carried dark circles underneath, and they look tired. I wish I could get them to go home to rest, but I understand why they won't. This guy has to wake up and quickly. How much longer can Ivey hold on, especially if she's injured? We have been here for hours.

I walk over to the guys and share the outcome of my meeting with Investigator Sullens. They smiled when they heard they could remain on the job, but I stressed the urgency in their reports. They agreed to handle it promptly.

A nurse walks into the room and asks for Deputy Brock Tuttle. With him positioned in the corner, she didn't notice him. He sat up in the chair when he heard his name, and they moved to the side of the waiting room so she could change his bandage. The nurse seems to take her time making the change. We watch as she dabs medicine on the wound. Tuttle turns and meets our stares, and his look means they want privacy. Could it be Tuttle has found a friend?

Tuttle spends twenty minutes with the nurse, and he produces a piece of paper with her name and number on it. "Before you ask, yes, she gave me her contact information. No, she's not dating anyone, and she hopes we find Agent Ivey." Tuttle slips the paper into his wallet and sits down next to Taylor with an enormous grin on his face.

We chuckle at Tuttle with his newfound love interest. What is the likelihood of us coworkers finding love amid a tragedy? I've heard of it happening before, but not in our South Georgia sheriff's office.

Lunchtime comes and goes without news. I am at the point of pulling my hair out. Living in a hospital waiting room is difficult at best. Without a shower in two days, I can only imagine how I smell. Frustration takes hold as we tell each other to go home and rest. No one leaves.

It is the middle of the afternoon, and a doctor pops his head into the room. "Your driver is Greg Leaver. Age 35. The address on his driver's license is in Alabama. We located no family members. The doctors are working on waking him from the coma, but he is still not coherent enough to answer questions. But a nurse sits in his room in case he improves. Greg's vitals are not stable, so we are monitoring him for internal bleeding. Hang tight, and someone will keep you updated."

"Bud, can you call the FBI and ask for a background check on our Greg Leaver? Maybe the background check will give us an idea of where he might be holding Ivey. I don't recall that last name before. So, I am taking a gamble, but I don't think he has any family around here. My guess is he picked our county on his way to somewhere else." I suggested as ideas race through my mind to nowhere.

"Yes, I am on it," Bud responds.

Taylor adds, "I am ready to beat the information out of Greg Leaver. If he hadn't taken Ivey, I would have aimed for the heart, not the gut."

"Taylor, please don't say that out loud. The GBI agent gave us a reprieve on the reports, and he allowed you and Tuttle to remain on the job while we search for Ivey. We can't jeopardize that by spouting off. I don't want you or anyone else under more scrutiny than what is necessary."

"Sorry, Sheriff. Patience is not my strong virtue, and finding Ivey is taking so long I am going stir crazy. Ivey is out there who knows where and in what condition."

Bud nods in agreement with me. "Ivey is the primary concern, but we can't step out of bounds. Not now. If Greg is the killer, and I think he is, and if he lives, he will never have the opportunity to be outside of a prison cell again. With the crimes he has committed, they should sentence him to the death penalty. I've testified once against a killer. One more time shouldn't matter. Only this time, I won't be testifying for a partner's murder. We will find Ivey." Bud states emphatically, and he believes it with all of his heart because it shows in his eyes. Bud doesn't think he will survive if he loses another partner. I hope, for his sake, he doesn't.

I step away from the guys and call the sheriff's office. Maggie answers on the first ring. She updates me on any issues at the office. The press calls continually, but Maggie reroutes their attention. The deputies tried to cover the county, but with two away, it is hard. I offer to call Captain Grayson and see if he can provide a staffer to handle patrol time overnight. Maggie makes notes expecting to need them. I update her on the driver's condition and ask Maggie to search the internet for Greg Leaver and call me with the results.

As I walk into the waiting room, Bud stands in the room's corner while Taylor and Tuttle sit side by side. Taylor holds his head in his hands as I sit on the other side of him. I place my hand on his shoulder, and we don't speak as there was no need. We are there for each other, and we both feel it.

A few minutes later, my phone rings. Maggie's number displays, "Sheriff, Maggie. I did as you requested with the internet search for Greg Leaver. You will not believe this, but he is a model consultant, or at least his website says he is a modeling consultant covering areas from Louisiana to Florida." Maggie clicked keys on the computer keyboard. "The site doesn't list any associates by name, but he mentions having associates in his bio.

"Unbelievable. That's it! Maggie, print everything on this guy, including the website information. I can't wait to tell the guys. Hopefully, this will perk them up. Thanks!"

Unable to contain my enthusiasm, I state, "Hey, guys. I've got news. Maggie did an internet search for our Greg Leaver, and he is a model consultant. Maggie is printing off information from his website. If he survives, we can get him by matching his DNA with the evidence on the shoes. Maggie is sending over a photo of Greg, too."

Taylor raises his head, and he has a smile on his face. "Are you for real, Sheriff? That's the best news I've heard since the doctors said Tuttle's injury was just a graze!"

Bud is already on his phone, barking orders to someone. I hear the words *photo, website, video,* and *evidence.* His mind is running along the same path as mine. If we can locate Greg's video in Tallahassee and any surrounding area, we can put him at the scene or at least in the crime's proximity.

A nurse walks into the room with an odd expression on her face and speaks with Bud. Bud looks around and catches my eye and gives me a slight head nod. I approach with apprehension. "Tell her what you told me, please," Bud states to the nurse.

"Sheriff, there is a guy at the nurse's station asking about Greg's condition. The guy claims to be a friend, and I thought you might want to meet him."

"Let's go get coffee, Bud. I hope he is still there, but I bet he is long gone by now."

The nurse heads back to the desk, and we follow a few seconds later. Of course, the guy is gone. We search the hallways and in Greg's room. "Bud, what are the odds this guy is working with Greg on his adventures?"

Bud pauses before he answers, "To tell you the truth, I hope he is. That gives me more hope that Ivey is still alive. Maybe this guy is the one keeping her alive."

"Since you stated it that way, I agree. Now, to see if the nurse can describe him enough for a sketch." I bounce my head up and down in agreement.

Bud steps up to the nurse's station and asks the nurse if she can ID Greg's visitor. She surprises us by taking a white piece of plain paper and sketches the visitor's face with a pencil from her desk. "A nurse and an artist. This is incredible. What color were his eyes and hair? Is there anything you noticed about his voice, height, weight, scars, tattoos? Anything that would be helpful?"

The nurse smiles at Bud as she states, "His eyes were brown as was his hair but light brown. He is about six feet and roughly 160 pounds, with no visible scars or tattoos. The visitor was nice looking, dressed in khakis and a navy-blue button-up shirt. I remember nothing extraordinary. He looks like your average joe."

"Another question—did he seem nervous to you?" Bud asks.

"As a matter of fact, he did. The visitor kept looking around while he spoke with me. But he was very polite, and he thanked me for my help."

We turn away from the desk then Bud abruptly turns back to the nurse and hands her his card. "Please call or text if you see him again."

With the card in hand, she replies, "It will be my pleasure."

This time we walk off, and I don't look back at the nurse, but I feel her eyes on my back as we stepped around the corner. Bud studies the sketch of the visitor. "I will send this to the office for an APB on the visitor. What about the news crews? Do you want to put it on TV?"

"If we release it to the press, then we will need to tell them about Ivey. I'm not sure I'm ready for that. But on the flip side, that would be a lot more people searching for her. What are your thoughts on the TV angle?" I am genuinely conflicted about the idea of releasing the sketch to the public. How would the citizens act if we told them there was a serial killer loose in our county?

"Let's ask Taylor and Tuttle for their opinions because we need more than just ours. Let's update them and see what their thoughts are about the TV." Bud's suggestion is best.

The walk back to the waiting room gives

me time to ponder the situation. Ivey is missing, the driver, Greg Leaver, is still unconscious, and an unknown visitor to the hospital has raised suspicions. Do I release the sketch to the media or just to the deputies? It would be nice to have more eyes searching for Ivey, but if the kidnapper has her locked away somewhere, no one has seen her anyway.

Taylor is pacing when we enter the waiting room. Tuttle sits with his head propped on the wall. It's obvious he feels miserable. He is still pale. Bud touches Tuttle on the shoulder before he speaks to him. Tuttle jumps up, "Is he awake?"

"Not yet, but we need to speak with you and Taylor. We can't decide what to do with recent information." Bud waits until Taylor sits in the chair next to Tuttle. "Greg had a visitor stop at the nurse's station. The duty nurse notified us, but we couldn't locate him when we made it back to her station. The nurse sketched the face of the visitor for us. Our dilemma is that we can't decide if we should release it to the deputies only or the media. Your input is important. We also hope that Ivey is still alive, especially with the visitor coming to the hospital for Greg."

"Think about it for a few minutes and give us your thoughts. If we release the sketch to the media, we will need to mention Ivey and her situation. That information will put the FBI in the hot seat and stir up the locals." I add, then continued, "do we want that on our plates too?"

"What are your thoughts about sharing the sketch, Bud? As Sheriff said, the FBI team will be the highlight of the news program," Taylor asks in a harsh tone.

"That's what we are trying to evaluate. I placed a call into my office to run the situation by a few people. Ultimately, the decision will be mine, and I must live with whatever choice I make." Bud says with a pained expression on his face.

I reach over and hold Bud's hand. The decision of a lifetime rests on his shoulders, and it means life or death for his partner. If it were my decision, I would say bring on the TV crew. I want as many people as I can get looking for Ivey. But then, I stop and think about it from another angle. Would anyone have seen Ivey with the kidnapper? He took her from her car in the pitch darkness while she drove alone. Would an offer of a reward help to drive home the urgency of the situation?

Greg has been in the hospital for over twenty-four hours, and he remains unconscious. Not only that, but Ivey's whereabouts are also still unknown. I see no other way to solve this other than bringing in the media unless we wait around until Greg wakes up—if he wakes up. But will it be too late for Ivey?

Just as we are preparing to notify the media, our nurse steps into the room to inform us Greg is stirring in the bed and mumbling. The doctor tried to get him to open his eyes, but he hasn't reacted to stimuli yet. The nurse gives us hope that Greg will come out of the coma in time to save Ivey and keep us from having to involve the media.

Taylor is beyond frustrated with sitting around and waiting. "Taylor, why don't you and Tuttle walk around and grab a snack? Bud and I will be here if anything changes. You will be the first to know."

"Yeah. Okay. Sheriff. Maybe a walk will do me good. Come on, Tuttle. Keep me company."

The guys retreat from the room and head outdoors. Taylor is losing hope of ever seeing Ivey again, and it is apparent in his demeanor. He's withdrawn, he isn't offering opinions on anything discussed, and Taylor always has an opinion on everything. It's hard to watch a friend hurt so bad, and there is nothing I can do but wait with him. I look at Bud and state, "I hope he recovers from this ordeal if Ivey doesn't make it out alive. He is really struggling."

Bud holds my hand and kisses it. "If he had taken you instead of Ivey, I'm not sure how I would handle it either. The anxiety of not knowing where you were would eat me alive. Taylor is a strong individual, and he has handled this situation well."

When Taylor and Tuttle enter the waiting room, Bud and I listen to Greg's nurse talk. The doctor suggests only two people visit

Greg and ask him questions. He is still out of it, but he continues to mumble the same sentence, and they can't understand it. "Bud and I will question Greg." I look at Tuttle and Taylor as I say it, then I turn to the nurse, " Can we go in now?"

Chapter 17

Taylor pushes us to go quickly before the doctor changes his mind. I glance at Bud, and we march off down the hallway to the ICU. Greg's nurse permits us entry to the room. What I see catches me a little off guard. Greg is younger than I expected. He is medium height, trim, and nice looking. The medical staff has hooked Greg up to every machine in the ICU. Blood runs through one device, IV bags hang from two different poles, and the heart monitor dings every so often.

Bud starts with the questions. "Greg, my name is FBI Special Agent Bud Dietrich, and I'm here with Sheriff Steele. Her deputies returned gunfire after you fired the first shot. Do you remember?"

A raspy sounding "Yes" comes out of Greg's mouth.

Bud continues, "we suspect you of murdering young girls in several states across the U.S. Did you kidnap Agent Ivey?"

Greg does not answer. He lies there with his eyes fluttering. After two minutes, the doctor comes over and checks his vitals. "His pulse is racing. The meeting will reconvene later. This pulse rate could send him into a heart attack or a stroke."

"Please, doc. Ask him yourself when he

settles down. Please. We have to find her."

"I'll do what I can, Sheriff, but it's really up to Greg. It's his choice to live or die. I've done all I can medically." The doctor turns towards his patient and pushes more medicine in his IV to calm his pulse.

Walking back to the waiting room, I glance at Bud. His emotions are in a twist. He either wants to cry or scream or both because Ivey has been missing almost 36 hours. If this hospital visitor isn't keeping her alive, Ivey won't last much longer without food and water.

The guys are pacing by the door when we turn the corner. When he sees our faces, Taylor knows the outcome of our conversation with Greg. He apparently thinks punching the wall is a better idea. I yell "No" a few seconds too late. Taylor's hand hits the wall, thankfully, between studs. "Taylor, what were you thinking? You could have broken your hand, and there would be no work for weeks. Go down to the ER and ask them to clean up your hand."

Taylor bows his head and strides off to the ER with blood dripping between his fingers. Tuttle runs over to him with paper towels and tries to wrap them. However, his hand is bleeding at such an alarming rate. The paper towels are no match. "Taylor, take the stairs. You need to be down there now. This is too much blood for the cut. You might have nicked an artery or something." I insist with urgency in my voice. "Hurry."

The nurse's station is calm when I walk up. Explaining that one of my deputies punched a hole in the waiting room wall is a little embarrassing. I advise them that the sheriff's office will pay for the damages. The nurse grins, "No need to act like this is the first time that's happened, Sheriff. There are patches from holes all over that room. I'll report it to the head nurse."

An attendant mops up Taylor's blood from the floor with a chemical mixture so strong. I feel like I am crying. When Bud sees me, he runs over, thinking something has happened. "I'm not crying, Bud. The cleaning solution is making my eyes water."

"Dilemma time—do we sit with Taylor or stay here for Greg?"

"Taylor has Tuttle. I'll ask him to stay with him, and we will remain here. I'm assuming they can stitch Taylor up. If not, we'll make other arrangements."

With my head laid back and my feet propped up in a chair, I'm sacked out when someone touches my leg. I barely open my eyes until I notice it is the doctor. "What's wrong?" I ask as I jump up.

"Greg semi-woke up, and I asked about Agent Ivey. He mumbled something that sounded like 'house.' I couldn't make out what the first word was, but the second, I'm reasonably sure it is house." The doctor's head bobbed up and down in his confidence.

"Bud, wake up, Bud." I nudge him. Then I shake him. Finally, he is alert enough for the play-by-play of the doctor's conversation with Greg.

"What do you make of that?" Bud asks.

"Ivey is in a warehouse. The one we searched the perimeter but couldn't gain access to. Well, I'm gaining access if I have to break the door down. Let's stop in the ER and check on Taylor before we go."

We take the stairs and locate Taylor and Tuttle standing in a doorway. Taylor looks horrible. It shocks me when I see how much gauze they wrapped around his hand. "What's the story on your hand?"

Taylor looks at it, "This was the stupidest thing I've done in a long time. I nicked an artery. The doctor stitched it together, and they wanted to give me blood. I begged that off. I'll remake my own. Where are you two headed?"

"We have an idea where they are holding Ivey. Greg woke up enough to mumble something that sounded like the word house. I'm betting on the warehouse. Want to ride? You can't do much, but at least you can be there for Ivey."

"Are you kidding? I injured my left hand, but I can do whatever we need with my right hand." Taylor says as he waves his right hand in the air.

"Tuttle, you in?"

"I'm in. I have an extra hand too. Let's go."

All four of us walk out of the emergency room with the goal of saving Ivey's life. I drive Taylor since they wrapped his hand, and Bud drives Tuttle. I can't decide if the guys should be here, but I don't have the heart to make them sit this one out. Taylor loves Ivey, and Tuttle is in it to finish it.

Our arrival at the warehouse is reserved without lights and no sirens. We pull in the lot across from the building with the box truck. The truck sits in the same spot. No movement comes from inside the warehouse, and the lights are off. Bud walks over to the door and pushes it open. "That's strange. I'll go in first, then you follow. Guys follow the Sheriff. No heroics. Put on your vests."

Two minutes pass, and everyone is suited up and ready for entry. Bud takes the lead, and the rest of us follow. The door is loud as it scratches the concrete floor. The smell is awful. It smells of mold and mildew. There are pallets of old food in the middle of the warehouse, and we watch big rats race to the exit as we pass. Bud points at some old rooms to one side of the warehouse. Our flashlights illuminate what used to be nice office spaces. The desks are still in place, as are phones, fax machines, and metal file cabinets.

The break room sits on the far side of the

building, across from our door. There are a table and chairs set up waiting for visitors. "This warehouse is creepy. It looks like people were here working one minute, and the next minute, they vanished," I tell the group, thinking I sure am glad I didn't search this building by myself.

"There are no noises and no noticeable footprints in the dust, other than ours. It appears to be empty. What's in the other warehouses out here?" Bud asks.

"I don't have a clue. I've never had a reason to suspect anything. The same owner probably owns them all if I have to guess. That's the guy who never returns a call. We will break into those buildings too and see what we find. If Ivey is here, we will find her."

Taylor exclaims, "Did you hear that? What is that noise, and where is it coming from?" He turns toward the door and runs. Tuttle is on his heels.

"Wait, Taylor. You can't go alone." I say to the back of Taylor's head as he leaves the building.

Bud and I run out of the warehouse and look both ways. Taylor and Tuttle vanished. "Where did they go, Bud? I told them to stay with us." I survey the surroundings trying to pick on a sound.

"This way. I vaguely hear a sound. Is it an air conditioner? Come on." Bud grabs my hand, and we run to another warehouse directly behind the original one. This one isn't as large, and the closer I get to it, I hear a motor churning.

Taylor and Tuttle peek in a window as we walk around the back of the building. "Sheriff, a man is standing next to a card table. He looks distraught and alone. I think he is talking on a cell phone. Can you or Bud look at him and see if this is the guy at the hospital? He fits the description." Taylor shares his observations.

Bud walks over to the window and glances inside. He holds up his phone with the sketch and compares it to the man inside, "That's him."

"Guys, we are going in. However, we don't know what to expect. There could be more people inside. Be ready for anything." I state as sweat runs down my back. This is what we've been waiting for, and we are ready to end it.

Bud places himself by the door. "If they lock the door, we will shoot, but if we do that, the guy will know we are here for him. Did anyone see another door?"

Tuttle answers, "Only a roll-up door."

"Good. We all stay here. Prepare for entry. On your call, Bud." I order.

With his fingers in the air, Bud counts down from three to one in under three seconds. When the third finger drops, the door flies open, and we run in with guns drawn. The man drops his phone and lets off several rounds from an AK47. He wasn't aiming, just trying to scare us.

We drop to the ground and skitter behind pallets. The pallets are large enough to accommodate two people at a time, but we can't see what the product is on the pallet. An AK47 can slice through most material. The gunman screams at us that we will never take him alive.

"That's your choice. However, the only way out is through us. If you lay your weapon down and get on your knees, we won't shoot. If you don't, you leave us no choice," Bud shouts.

There is a deafening silence in the warehouse until we hear a faint scraping sound coming from upstairs. "Time is up. If Agent Ivey is in the warehouse, she will need medical attention. What's your decision?" I shout, unwilling to wait for long.

The hospital visitor shouts more demands about Greg's release and the need for a vehicle. Bud shouted back, no deal. Then we sat in silence for a few seconds. We heard movement and lifted our heads so we could see over the pallets.

The gunman reaches out as if he is laying his gun down when in a quick second, he turns the gun on himself and blows the top of his head across the room. "I guess he didn't like his options," I say as I run towards the dilapidated staircase in the back of the warehouse. Bud is right behind me and then Taylor. Tuttle stays at the bottom. He stood next to the dead guy, but he watched us as we walked up the rickety steps.

As soon as I find her, I scream, "Bud, Taylor, Ivey is here. Call EMS. They need to hurry." When I enter the room, I see that someone chained her to a rusted metal pole. It takes both Bud and Taylor to remove the chain. Ivey is semiconscious, and she moans as the guys move her. Bud sits on the floor and holds her like a baby. One of her eyes is swollen shut, and there are cuts and bruises over most of her body. Looking at her, I don't see any visible broken bones, but who knows until she gets x-rays. Taylor sits next to Bud and rubs her hair. It is the saddest and sweetest gesture I've ever seen.

The ambulance turns into the lot, and I step out on the stairway, landing to meet them. Tuttle shows the EMS guys the way. "Be careful on the stairs. They are not sturdy. If you need help getting the gurney up, yell."

EMS attendants assess Ivey's injuries quickly. Their diagnosis begins with dehydration, semiconsciousness, and a possible concussion with low vital signs. Ivey wears a neck brace as a precaution as they transport her to the hospital within minutes of arrival. Bud insists on riding with Ivey to the hospital. Taylor rides with me as we follow them.

Tuttle volunteers to clean up the warehouse scene. He works with the crime scene techs and the medical examiner's office to secure the scene and collect enough evidence to convict Greg of kidnapping and murder. We will run the dead guy's fingerprints for his ID, and we will also list him for kidnapping and murder.

Back in the hospital waiting room, I realize how much I detest this room. We've been in here for too many hours recently. I had just ended a call when Bud walks out of the emergency room treatment area to find us. "Ivey is in critical condition. The doctors are taking her for a CT scan of her brain. She may have a brain bleed. The neurosurgeon spotted a concave area on the back of her head. They fear the concave area is causing her to lose consciousness. If she has one, the doctors will perform surgery to release the pressure."

"Oh, no. I can't believe what this guy does to his victims. Tuttle stayed back to work the crime scene. He says the techs found usable evidence against both men. So, at least, we can watch Greg go to prison for life or the death row."

"Greg has to live long enough for the conviction. I'm stepping outside to call the FBI office to give them an update. Come get me if there are changes while I'm out." Bud states in a depressed tone. He walks out the doors with his head down and shoulders slumped.

Glancing at Taylor, I see him sitting with his head is in his hands. If he leans over any further, he will be on the floor. I move over into a different chair and place my hand on his shoulder. "Taylor, she'll be fine. She's healthy and strong. Have faith."

"Sheriff, I'm trying, but being scared, mad, tired, and worried makes it hard to have faith. I don't want to lose her." Taylor shares.

"You won't lose her. Ivey will endure recovery time, both physical and mental, but she is a survivor. You'll see." Taylor turns silent again. Is he thinking about Ivey's chances of not wanting a man's relationship because of her experiences? That would concern me, too, if I were in his place. Ivey is the only one that can provide that answer.

Tuttle enters the waiting room a few hours later with a green pallor on his face. "Say nothing. I feel horrible. The stench in the warehouse finally made me sick. Then I was in the deceased's vicinity when they scraped his splayed body parts into a baggie."

"Thanks for the visuals, Tuttle," Taylor says in a testy tone.

"I, for one, appreciate you handling the scene so we can be here. Ivey is in surgery now. They think she has a brain bleed. We should hear something soon from the surgeon."

"Bud was talking on his phone as I came in. How is he holding up?" Tuttle asks, concerned.

"He is doing okay. He is worried about Ivey, no doubt, but holding his own. Bud is calling the FBI office to give them an update while Ivey is in surgery. He is trying to keep busy."

The guys nod their heads in agreement. Taylor leans back in his chair while Tuttle lays his head against the wall, then they both close their eyes. The whole ordeal exhausted everyone, and we are ready for it to be over. Greg is in the hospital, and his accomplice is dead. Surely, we can find enough evidence to convict Greg for all the murders. Bud will share what happened here with the other FBI agents and try to connect the killings' time frame. Like I told Taylor, we must have faith.

Several hours later, the surgeon finds us in the waiting room in the same chairs as before, dozing. "Sheriff," I vaguely hear someone call my name. Then I feel a tap on my shoulder. I jump up, not remembering where I am.

"Sheriff. I'm here for an update on Agent Ivey." The doctor states.

"I'm sorry. You startled me." I call out to everyone to wake up, and once we are alert, the doctor proceeds.

"Agent Ivey is resting in ICU so that we can keep close tabs on her. She remains unconscious, but that will subside in the coming days. Agent Ivey had a small brain bleed, and the surgeon stopped it. They roughed agent Ivey up pretty bad, but she has no broken bones and no internal bleeding. With time, she should make a 100% recovery."

Taylor nudges me in the back. I turn and read his face, and I realize what I must ask. "Doctor, was Agent Ivey sexually abused by these men?"

"No, Sheriff. The rape kit was negative. Which, of course, is a good thing for her recovery. Two at a time can visit her. Once she moves to a regular room, you can stay overnight with her. Go to the double door and press the intercom when you want to enter."

"Thanks, Doctor. Bud and Taylor, you visit first. I'll see her on the visitation round."

"Sheriff, are you sure?" Taylor asks with an anxious tone. He wants to see her so badly, he shivers.

"Yes, Taylor. I'm sure. Go on, you two. I'll be here when you finish."

Chapter 18

Both men turn and leave me standing in the waiting room. Now, alone, I call Maggie. It delights her that Agent Ivey is on the road to recovery. We have received no news yet about the evidence collected at the warehouse. Maggie shares the best news for our group. Doc James confirmed the gun found in the box truck matches the size of the girl's wounds. The gun also provided unmistakable fingerprints of Greg Leaver. Then she stated. I have several messages from the news stations. Thinking about handling those, I tell Maggie we will hold a news conference in the coming days to cover all the details.

Ten minutes pass, and the men return to the waiting room. "The nurse with Ivey stated she is waking herself up. She's having bouts of dreams where she mumbles. They only let us stay a little while," Taylor explains.

"Well, Taylor, it looks like Ivey will be fine once she can pull herself out of the coma. She is one lucky lady with all she endured during her captivity. How's the hand?" I look down at his wrapped hand.

"It's better. My fingers move now. The stitches come out in two days. Tuttle's stitches come out this afternoon. Both of us will be back to normal in no time," Taylor explains, wiggling his fingers.

"That's great! The sheriff's office could use a full force again. Some of our guys are working non-stop," I share, and then I told the guys about the gun and the fingerprints. We fist bump with each other in celebration.

"Since the GBI cleared us, we are working our regular shifts tomorrow. The patrol deputies can get some relief. I bet they are exhausted too," Tuttle states.

Bud stands and says, "I'm going for a shower and something to eat. I also need to follow up on the evidence collection. There must be enough to convict Greg. What was his motivation for the kidnapping, and why the warehouse? He came close to killing several officers. We can't let him walk out!"

"I agree, Bud. I'm staying until I can see Ivey. Go shower at home, and we will meet up later."

"Home? That sounds good." Bud leans down and kisses me in front of Taylor and Tuttle.

"I knew it! Ivey said you two would make it work. Now, I hope we get the chance," Taylor gets up from his chair and grins at me.

"You will, Taylor, you will."

The men walk out of the room and leave me with my thoughts. The possibility of Ivey being my sister still nags at me. I want the answer, and the only way to do that is DNA. With a plan in mind, I call Doc James and explain my idea. He agrees to it, now, to get Ivey to agree.

While I wait the hour until the next scheduled ICU visitation, I ponder my approach with Ivey. Does she feel the same way I do when we were together? From the moment I met her, I felt like we have known each other for years. We favor each other in our mannerisms and looks. I will convince her when I show her Dad's handwriting on the back of the photo.

A nurse calls me back to Ivey's room. Ivey is trying to pull out of the coma, but she is fighting the nurses. They ask me to talk to her to calm her.

"Ivey, it's Sheriff Steele. I'm here. We are waiting for you to come back to us. Calm down and let the nurses tend to you. Don't fight us." As I speak, I rub her arm. Ivey calms down enough for the nurses to treat her. Then, I watch the machines connected to her beep and bounce across the screen. Her blood pressure and pulse continue to soar. "Ivey, calm down. Calm down. Rest your body. You're safe now. We got the killers."

The moment I tell her we have the bad guys, everything changes. She drifts off to sleep. Her blood pressure and pulse drop to normal levels, and she calms. "I guess she needed to know the outcome. Hopefully, she will rest now."

"Thanks for being here, Sheriff Steele. She needs her rest now."

"I'm going home for a shower and then to the office, but I'll return this afternoon. If anything changes, please call my cell phone." I hand the nurse a business card with the cell phone number circled in red and walk out of the room.

The next few hours are a fury of activity. My desk resembles an explosion. I put things in stacks, and when Bud pops in, I ask him, "Any word on the evidence yet?"

"Nothing yet. The crime scene techs are working on it now. Probably another two hours before we have any results. Any change in Ivey?"

Explaining the situation at the hospital, I watch as Bud's expression changes from concern to relief when I finish. "She'll be fine now. She had to make certain everyone was okay, and we got the bad guys. I didn't tell Ivey a bad guy killed himself, not yet anyway."

"I didn't tell her either. We can share that information when she is stronger. The nurse on duty has my cell phone if there is a change. I need to get a little work in while we wait."

Bud indicates he will go to the hospital and hang out in the waiting room. "I'll call you later." Bud walks out of my office with his shoulders slumped. Worry and exhaustion cause that reaction in people.

I jump into the issues on my desk with both feet. And it takes both feet to get through them. There is a mound of patrol reports that need my approval before releasing them and then phone calls to make to a few county citizens. The citizen calls stem from some young drivers drag racing, and always this time of year, I assure the callers I will stop the activity.

By late afternoon, I grow weary sitting in my chair. I call Bud, and he doesn't answer, so I try Taylor. No answer. My nerves get the best of me, so I drive to the hospital. I stroll into an empty waiting room. Pushing the button for the ICU, I notice my hand shakes. The nurse is apologetic when she meets me at the door. Agent Ivey woke up thirty minutes ago, and Bud and Taylor are with her. They are preparing her to move to a regular room. The nurse steps aside and suggests I join the guys.

When I enter Ivey's room, our eyes met, and tears flow. We can't stop them. I walk over and hug her, then sit on the edge of her bed. When I look around, I notice that the guys bolted from the room. I guess tears will do that. Ivey talks about her ordeal, and I listen. I ask no questions as I give her time to talk. Ivey finally asks about her captor, and I can't withhold the outcome, so I tell her he committed suicide when we entered the warehouse. Ivey seems to take the information in stride. After a few minutes of alone time, I bring the guys back into the room. We sit with her until she grows sleepy.

As we are leaving the hospital, Bud's

phone rings. He glances at me then raises his finger as he steps to the side of the walkway. Taylor and I pause in our tracks too. We've been waiting on that call. We gave the district attorney plenty of evidence to send Greg to prison. The evidence includes prints from the candy wrapper and shoe and the girls' phones and purses found in the warehouse. All of which had Greg's fingerprints on them. Video surveillance from Tallahassee places him at the cheerleading competition too. The most critical piece of evidence lies in the hospital bed above our heads. FBI Agent Ivey will be the lead witness.

Bud paces as he listens. He asked a few questions of the district attorney. Taylor's eyebrows bunch together, the look he gives when worry wins. I won't be able to hold him back from killing Greg if the justice system doesn't prevail. I turned to Bud as he is ending the call. He turns to face us. "We got him. We provided overwhelming evidence against Greg. He will remain in the jail ward until his health allows him a trip to jail. The district attorney is proceeding with charges now." The three of us hug and then celebrate with a steak dinner. Afterward, Taylor goes back to the hospital, and Bud and I drive home.

The morning sun wakes me up bright and early, and today is the day. I plan on speaking with Ivey about my suspicions. Doc James is on standby if she agrees to the DNA test.

Showered, dressed, and fed, I let Bud sleep, but I left a note on the kitchen counter. Ivey is bright-eyed when I enter her room. "Why the apprehensive look, Sheriff? Everything okay?"

"Yes, everything is fine. I would like to discuss something with you if you are up for it."

"Sure. Go ahead." Ivey stirs in the bed, trying to find a comfortable position.

"Since we met each other, I've had a strange sensation we know each other. Our mannerisms are similar, your handwriting is like Dad's, and your last name is my middle name."

"Are you saying we might be related? The handwriting scene in your office. That's why you stopped talking. You knew then, didn't you?" Ivey asks, then continues, "So, your name is Jada Ivey Steele?"

"Yes, that's my name, spelled like yours too. When you introduced yourself to me, your name shocked me, but we were so busy, it took a while for me to put it all together. Then your handwriting was familiar, but I couldn't remember from where I saw it. It had been a while since I had looked at Dad's, but when you asked about the picture at my house and Dad had written the date on the back, it confirmed it for me."

"Why did you wait to say something? I hope we are. That would be incredible."

"I guess I was a little scared, not

knowing how you would react," I said with a grin.

"You would be my first pick for a relative! It makes sense why you think we are related. You grew up with a dad, and I grew up with a mom. Could we be sisters?"

"I'm not sure, but Doc James is on standby if you would agree to a DNA test. Doc James can do the test in his office within a couple of days." I pleaded.

"Call him. Let's get the test started. Who would have thought a serial killer would bring us together?" Ivey grins as she thinks about the possibility.

I place the call to Doc James, and he says he will be over in thirty minutes. He will draw blood from both of us and start the testing this afternoon. My stomach flutters at the thought Ivey might be my sister.

Ivey continues to get stronger with therapy and IVs. She remains in the hospital but in much better spirits. Taylor stays with her most of the time when he is not on duty. Nightmares plague her sleep, but her doctor tells her those should subside with time.

We tied a nice tight bow around the case for Greg Leaver's conviction as our kidnapper and killer. But we found a connection we weren't expecting. The warehouse and box truck owner, Stuart Milton Boards, is Greg's cousin. The dead warehouse guy turned out to be Greg's childhood friend, and Greg confessed his role along with Stuart's as the masterminds of the operation when we presented our evidence. Stuart Boards sits in prison, waiting his turn for trial. That was a fun call with the Lamar County Sheriff because he wasn't happy with the outcome.

The ordeal started with a few girls for a big corporate party because Stuart wanted to impress his international business associates. The businessmen requested young girls be at their side for the night, and Stuart made it happen. Stuart contacted Greg, and they devised a plan. Once ready, they set the plan in motion. After the first event occurred, they continued their arrangement with Stuart funding the escapades, and it grew by increasing contact with girls through social media. They never intended to murder, but they couldn't get caught either. So, the chase continued, as did the murders. Greg can't fathom how his plan went so wrong. He kept asking how we found him? He never once asked about Agent Ivey. This is one trial I can't wait to happen.

Two days after Doc James begins the test, he calls my cell phone while Bud, Taylor, and I visit Ivey. I answer the call as my pulse races, and it ends with a huge grin on my face. Hugging Ivey, I ask, "Where do we go from here, Sis?"

New Release Coming August 2021!

Torched gun stores and the store owners burned alive. Who would do something this horrible? What do they have to gain?

Flames from a torched gun store bounce across the rooftop, consuming everything in its wake. With the heat from the fire, bullets fly through the night air as the firestarter watches the scene. This is his first.

FBI Agents Mac and Spencer join a task force with ATF and an Atlanta PD fire investigator to stop the gun store torcher. The firestarter strikes as he travels Interstate 75. The fires demolish stores and burn people alive as the firestarter feeds a need.

How many stores will he torch before the FBI stops him? How many people will he murder?

Follow the case to see how everything comes together for a shocking ending!

Books by A.M. Holloway

MOA (Mac Morris Thriller Book 1)

Pieces of Murder (Digger Collins Thriller Book 1)

~~~~~~~~~~~~~~~

Visit **www.amholloway.com** to sign up for my reader's list and updates!

Made in the USA
Las Vegas, NV
03 August 2022

52612786R00152